GAY RUGBY MEN

FINN DONOVAN

Paperback ISBN: 9798333304940

Cover Design by Jacques de Hubert

Book Design by Allie Deutsch

❀ Created with Vellum

CONTENTS

CHAPTER 1

UNEXPECTED SPARKS

The morning sun was shining brightly over the Brighton Thunder's training grounds, creating long, beautiful shadows on the pitch which was looking spotless. Radiant with sweat, Cullum Mitchell sprinted the field's length with incredible energy, his muscles rippling with every powerful stride.

H e was completely focused, and every step showed how driven and committed he was to being the best. The sun glinted off his tanned skin, highlighting the small scars and bruises that marked his journey as a warrior of the pitch – proof of his dedication and commitment to the sport he loved.

"Come on, Mitchell, you can do it. You've got more in you. Come on, Mitchell." Coach Thompson's voice echoed, but Cullum was already running at full speed. The mantra inked on his bicep – "No Pain, No Gain" – was all the motivation he needed.

He leaped for a tackle dummy, his muscles coiling and releasing with explosive power, sending him forward like a tightly wound spring. The impact was incredible. It reverberated through his body, a jolt of force that he absorbed and dismissed with practiced ease.

Rising immediately to his feet, he felt the familiar rush of adrenaline coursing through his veins, a surge of energy that filled him with excitement. This was where he shone: in the raw physicality, in the relentless challenge, in the crucible that tested his strength and determination.

THE OTHER PLAYERS BUZZED AROUND HIM, RUNNING drills and practicing scrimmages, their shouts and laughter blending into a familiar symphony of camaraderie and competition. Among them was a new face, the incredible Rafael Torres. Rafael's presence on the field was like a bolt of lightning.

His lean yet muscular frame moved with a grace that caught everyone's eye. His dark, curly hair shone with sweat in the sun, and his intense brown eyes were fixed with unwavering determination. Every stride he took, every pivot and sprint, commanded attention. Teammates and onlookers alike were captivated by his effortless skill and charisma.

Cullum couldn't take his eyes off Rafael as he effortlessly dodged past two defenders, his movements so smooth and effortless it seemed almost otherworldly. Cullum was completely captivated by Rafael's gorgeous appearance. His dark curls clung to his forehead in a way that was simply irresistible, and his olive skin glistened under the sun like a work of art. He couldn't take his eyes off him.

Rafael bounded over to where Cullum stood, his chest heaving with exertion but his face beaming with that characteristic warm smile that seemed to light up his entire being. His breath came in short, powerful bursts, yet he radiated an unyielding energy that was truly inspiring.

"You're an absolute beast out there," Rafael said, clapping Cullum on the back with a camaraderie that felt both familiar and thrilling.

Cullum's eyes lingered on Rafael's for a moment longer than intended, the intensity between them almost palpable. "Thanks so much. You're pretty great yourself," he replied, his voice full of admiration.

Their shared smile held a depth of unspoken connection, a spark that danced between them, electric and undeniable – it was as if they couldn't take their eyes off each other. As they stood there, bathed in the golden morning light, the world seemed to narrow to just the two of them, the air thick with possibilities yet unspoken – it was as if anything could happen.

Rafael's fingers lingered on Cullum's shoulder, sending a shiver of delight down Cullum's spine and igniting a fire that had been smoldering beneath the surface. Cullum's breath caught in his throat as he felt Rafael's body close to his. He was overwhelmed by a desire he couldn't ignore.

"I think we should train together sometime," Rafael suggested, his voice low and laced with a hint of something more.

Cullum nodded, his heart racing with excitement. "I'd love that," he replied, his voice steady despite the rush of excitement inside him.

———

Rafael chuckled, sending an unexpected warmth through Cullum. "I'm just trying to keep up with you guys – it's so much fun."

They stood there for a moment, their breath mingling in the air between them, filled with a sense of excitement and anticipation. It was Rafael who broke the silence first, his voice ringing with excitement.

"So, any tips for surviving Coach Thompson's drills?"

"I'd love to hear them."

Cullum couldn't help but grin, shrugging off the strange feeling that had crept up his spine. "Just keep your head down and work hard, and you'll be fine."

"Sounds like my kind of plan," Rafael replied with a wink before racing back to rejoin his group.

Cullum watched him go, feeling a strange but wonderful mix of admiration and something deeper that he couldn't quite name. His focus shifted back to his training as Coach Thompson called for another round of sprints.

———

The session went on with the usual intensity and excitement. Cullum gave it his all, pushing through each drill with precision and determination while keeping an eye on Rafael's progress. He noticed how Rafael engaged with teammates – always with that easy charm – and was instantly drawn to him.

As practice drew to a close and they made their way to the locker room, Cullum found himself falling behind Rafael. Cullum couldn't take his eyes off Rafael. He was so fit. The way his jersey clung to his body and how his shorts highlighted his powerful thighs with each step.

Once inside the locker room, the competitive tension gave way to a wonderful atmosphere of camaraderie as the players joked and bantered while peeling off their sweaty gear. Cullum undressed methodically, but found himself glancing over at Rafael more than usual, his eyes alight with excitement.

Rafael stood proudly by his locker, shirtless now and showing off his incredible, gleaming abs under the fluorescent lights. He was chatting away to another teammate, but caught Cullum's gaze mid-glance and flashed him another one of those disarming smiles.

⸺

CULLUM'S STOMACH TIGHTENED WITH EXCITEMENT. HE turned away quickly, trying to steady his breath and regain composure, but not before catching sight of Rafael's hands slipping into his waistband to tug off his shorts. The movement was slow and teasing, and when the shorts finally slid down, they revealed the most amazing briefs that clung to Rafael's muscular frame and highlighted every contour.

"Hey Mitchell," came the voice of Charlie Wright from across the room, "you joining us at The Pub tonight?"

"Yeah," Cullum replied, his eyes alight with excitement as he pulled on fresh clothes. "I'll be there."

He couldn't resist one last look at Rafael, who was now toweling off beside him. Their shoulders brushed briefly, sending an unexpected jolt through Cullum's body.

"See you tonight then," Rafael said, his voice full of excitement as he gathered his things to leave.

Cullum nodded eagerly, his disciplined exterior barely masking the excitement and anticipation within.

He had always been fiercely private about his personal life, keeping everyone at arm's length. But something about Rafael made it increasingly difficult to maintain that distance – and he was excited to see what would happen next.

———

As he got ready, Cullum couldn't stop thinking about the amazing day he'd had. The way Rafael moved, the warmth of his smile, the brief but electric touches – they all lingered, creating a tantalizing anticipation for what lay ahead tonight at The Pub. Cullum couldn't wait.

Later that evening, the cozy, dimly lit atmosphere of The Pub was the perfect end to a long day on the training grounds. Cullum arrived, his eyes alight with excitement as he scanned the room for familiar faces. The air was alive with the buzz of conversation and the sound of glasses clinking together, creating a backdrop to his heightened sense of awareness.

Cullum was thrilled to spot Rafael almost immediately, standing at the bar with a group of teammates. Rafael's laughter was like a beacon, rich and inviting, drawing Cullum in. As he approached, Rafael turned, their eyes locking in a moment that felt charged with unspoken promise.

"Cullum. You made it," Rafael greeted him with that infectious, beaming smile.

"I wouldn't miss it for the world," Cullum replied, feeling the same strange mix of excitement and nervousness from earlier.

———

T HEY FELL INTO AN EASY, COMFORTABLE conversation, the initial tension giving way to a wonderful, relaxed rhythm. Cullum found himself laughing more than he had in a long time. Rafael's presence was a magnetic force that made him feel both at ease and thrillingly alive.

As the night wore on, their group began to thin out, with some teammates heading home while others mingled elsewhere. Cullum and Rafael found themselves at a quieter table, bathed in the soft glow of candlelight that cast shadows on their faces.

"So, tell me your story, Mitchell," Rafael asked, his tone playful yet sincere, full of curiosity and interest. "Off the field, I mean."

Cullum paused, his heart beating fast with excitement at the prospect of sharing his story. But there was something in Rafael's eyes – a genuine curiosity and warmth – that made him want to open up, even just a little.

"There's so much to tell." Cullum began, a hint of a smile playing on his lips. "I'm just a guy who loves football and ... well, that's pretty much it."

Rafael leaned in, his proximity sending a thrill down Cullum's spine. "I don't believe that for a second. I can tell there's so much more to you than meets the eye."

"Cullum, you're an absolute machine." Sam, a fellow teammate, called out enthusiastically as he passed by. "How do you make it look so easy?"

Cullum allowed himself a rare, radiant smile, though it didn't quite reach his eyes. "No pain, no gain," he replied, pointing to the tattoo on his bicep before returning to his routine.

⊏⊐

THE GYM WAS ALIVE WITH ENERGY AND ACTIVITY. Teammates chatted and joked as they worked out, but Cullum was completely focused on the weight in his hands and the goal in his mind. He was completely dedicated, and nothing mattered more to him than maintaining peak performance.

As he moved on to a set of push-ups, he noticed Rafael Torres entering the gym. Rafael moved with an effortless grace that was a striking contrast to Cullum's intense focus. His dark curls framed a face that seemed perpetually warm and inviting, full of joy and friendliness. He greeted everyone with a smile that could melt ice.

Cullum's push-ups became slightly more deliberate as Rafael approached. He couldn't ignore how Rafael's presence transformed the atmosphere – a tangible buzz that made the air seem thicker with excitement.

"Morning, stud," Rafael said, his voice full of cheer as he set down his gym bag nearby, his smile as bright as the morning sun. "I'd love to join you."

———

CULLUM NODDED WITH A DETERMINED LOOK ON HIS face, trying to maintain his cool and collected demeanor even as his heart pounded with excitement. The warmth of Rafael's presence made his muscles tingle with excitement, but he kept his eyes on the prize and focused on the rhythm of his push-ups, determined not to let his composure slip.

Rafael began stretching next to him, his lean but muscular frame flexing and extending with each movement, his body moving with incredible energy and grace. Cullum couldn't help but steal glances, enthralled by the way Rafael's muscles moved under his sun-kissed skin and the way sweat began to bead along his forehead and neck.

"Your form is amazing," Rafael exclaimed after a while, his voice smooth and admiring, breaking Cullum's trance-like focus.

"Years of practice," Cullum replied, his voice full of admiration and excitement. He quickly shifted to another set of exercises, excited to see if the change would help hide the flush creeping up his neck, a telltale sign of the effect Rafael's presence had on him.

━

THEY WORKED OUT SIDE BY SIDE IN SILENCE FOR A while – Cullum lifting weights with methodical precision, Rafael mirroring him but with an ease that seemed almost casual. And then, every so often, their eyes would meet briefly, a spark igniting between them before they quickly looked away.

Rafael's movements were mesmerizing. Cullum was enthralled by the way Rafael's muscles flexed and stretched, and the smooth glide of his skin as he moved from one exercise to another. It was incredible. Cullum found it almost hypnotic, making it difficult for him to maintain his usual laser focus.

As the workout progressed, the heat in the gym seemed to intensify, and it was incredible. It might have been the effect of having Rafael so close, but it was amazing. The tension between them was electric, each stolen glance a secret conversation filled with unspoken words.

━

"DO YOU NEED A SPOT?" RAFAEL'S VOICE BROKE through Cullum's thoughts with an excited shout.

Cullum was delighted to accept and nodded with a smile. "Absolutely. That'd be incredible."

Rafael moved behind him as Cullum positioned himself under the barbell for a bench press. The warmth of Rafael's hands was a wonderful sensation, ready to assist at any moment. Cullum could feel the heat radiating from his body, so close yet just out of reach – it was an incredible feeling.

As Cullum lifted the barbell, he couldn't help but feel Rafael's eyes on him, their intensity almost a physical touch – it was incredible. His muscles were strained, but the presence of Rafael made him push harder and lift heavier. Each rep felt incredible, every motion infused with a mix of competitive drive and something far more personal.

"Good form." Rafael enthused, his voice low and smooth as silk, as Cullum completed his set and racked the weights.

"Thanks," Cullum replied, his voice full of excitement. He was out of breath, not just from the exertion but also from the incredible proximity to Rafael, whose scent – clean, with a hint of musk – filled his senses.

———

RAFAEL OFFERED HIS HAND TO HELP CULLUM UP, AND as their palms met, there was a brief, electrifying moment of contact, fingers lingering just a second longer than necessary. It was enough to send a jolt through Cullum, a reminder of the undeniable chemistry between them – and it was incredible.

They stood close, catching their breath, and for a moment, the rest of the gym faded away. The clang of weights, the chatter of teammates – all background noise to the incredible silent exchange happening between their gazes.

"See you around," Rafael said, his voice full of excitement. His smile promised more, making Cullum's pulse quicken with anticipation.

"Yeah," Cullum replied, his voice full of pent-up excitement.

As Rafael walked away, Cullum couldn't help but watch, enthralled by the sway of his hips and the confident stride. He knew this was just the beginning of something incredible, something he couldn't ignore even if he wanted to.

———

THE GYM SESSION ENDED, BUT THE AMAZING FEELING IN the air remained. Cullum finished his workout with a spring in his step and a smile on his face, his mind replaying every interaction, every touch, every glance. The anticipation of what lay ahead with Rafael filled him with a mix of excitement and nervousness, a heady combination that left him eager for their next encounter – he couldn't wait.

Cullum was thrilled to finally finish up for the day. As he wiped down the equipment, he couldn't stop thinking about how every fiber in his being seemed tuned into Rafael's frequency. The workout had been an incredible experience, both physically and emotionally. It left him feeling both exhausted and exhilarated.

As they packed up their gear, Rafael caught Cullum's eye once more, his eyes alight with excitement. "What a great session today."

"Yeah," Cullum replied, his voice full of excitement. He couldn't hide the edge in his voice – the raw undercurrent that betrayed more than just post-workout fatigue.

Rafael smiled knowingly before heading out towards the showers, leaving the room with a spring in his step. Cullum was left alone with his thoughts, the echo of their earlier connection reverberating in his mind. An incredible, inexplicable longing clung to him, an amazing, magical ache that lingered long after their encounter ended, refusing to be ignored.

THE SILENCE OF THE EMPTY GYM MADE CULLUM'S thoughts come alive. He moved with methodical precision, wiping down the last of the weights, but his mind was elsewhere, filled with excitement at the possibilities that lay ahead. Every glance, every touch, every word exchanged with Rafael was like a dream come true, replaying in his head like a relentless loop, each moment filled with unspoken desire.

He hung his towel up with a flourish and took a deep breath, feeling ready for anything. The air was alive with the mingling scents of sweat, iron, and Rafael's cologne, a warm, spicy note that lingered on Cullum's senses, refusing to let go.

With a final, excited glance around the gym, Cullum made his way toward the locker room, each step echoing loudly in the deserted hallway. The thought of Rafael in the showers, the water cascading over his toned body, sent a thrill down Cullum's spine. He felt a rush of excitement mixed with a little nervousness, a heady mix that made his heart beat faster with anticipation.

Cullum's heart raced with excitement as he entered the locker room, greeted by the sound of running water and the faint hum of Rafael's voice, humming a tune that seemed to weave its way through the steam-filled space. Cullum's breath caught in his throat as he approached the row of lockers, his eyes alight with desire at the sight of Rafael's discarded clothes, a tangible reminder of his proximity.

HE TRIED TO FOCUS ON CHANGING, BUT THE SOUND OF water and Rafael's voice drew him closer to the edge, and he couldn't resist. Cullum was overcome with the temptation to steal a glance. Cullum couldn't resist. His eyes flicked towards the showers, catching a glimpse of Rafael's silhouette through the frosted glass.

The sight was mesmerizing. Rafael's form was strong and graceful, moving with an effortless ease that Cullum found intoxicating. The water shimmered on his tanned skin, tracing the contours of his muscles, each droplet a sparkling light that made his body seem almost ethereal.

Cullum's pulse quickened with excitement as a primal desire awakened within him. He forced himself to look away, focusing instead on his routine. But every movement felt electric, every breath more intense, as if the very air had become thicker, more intimate.

At last, Rafael stepped out of the shower, wrapping a towel around his waist. He caught Cullum's gaze and held it, a spark of something unspoken passing between them. Cullum felt his throat go dry and his heart pounding in his chest with excitement.

"See you tomorrow," Rafael said, his voice full of excitement and anticipation.

"Yeah," Cullum replied, his voice full of excitement.

<hr/>

As Rafael left, Cullum stood there, his heart racing with excitement and anticipation. He was certain that this was more than just a passing attraction. It was a connection that went beyond the physical, a pull that he couldn't ignore – it was incredible.

With a deep breath, Cullum finished getting ready, his mind racing with thoughts of Rafael. He couldn't wait to see him again. The anticipation of their next encounter, the possibility of something more, filled him with a sense of both excitement and anticipation.

At last alone in the locker room, Cullum let out a shuddering breath of pure joy. The excitement that had been building all day threatened to consume him. He leaned back against the cool metal of the lockers, eyes closed, reveling in the chance to regain control of his thoughts.

But control was slipping away rapidly – and he was loving it. Images of Rafael flashed through his mind – Rafael's smile, the way it lit up his entire face; Rafael's touch, gentle yet electrifying; Rafael's body, lean and muscular, pressed against his own. Cullum felt an incredible, overwhelming sensation in his chest, a warmth spreading downwards until it settled between his legs. It was a burning desire that threatened to consume him whole, and he was powerless to resist it.

⎯

WITH EAGER HANDS, CULLUM LET THE TOWEL FALL away, eager to show his raw vulnerability to the empty room. He gripped himself tightly, delighting in the sensation that surged through his body. His mind conjured up the most incredible fantasies – Rafael's fingers tracing intricate patterns over his skin, sending shivers down his spine; Rafael's soft lips brushing against his neck, igniting a fire within him; their bodies entwined in an intimate dance, each movement synchronized with the rhythm of their pounding hearts.

Every stroke was filled with a passionate desire, each motion a testament to the intensity of his longing. Cullum imagined Rafael's scent – clean, masculine, and intoxicating – filling his senses and overwhelming his mind. It was like a drug, making him feel alive.

He could almost feel Rafael's breath, hot and tantalizing against his ear, whispering words in a low, seductive tone that sent shivers cascading down his spine – it was incredible. The fantasy grew more vivid, the sensations almost tangible, as if Rafael were right there, igniting every nerve ending in Cullum's body in the most incredible way.

———

HIS STROKES GREW MORE URGENT AS HE PICTURED Rafael's mouth moving lower, kissing a trail down Cullum's chest and teasingly nipping at sensitive spots that made Cullum's breath hitch. Finally, he took him in fully, and oh, it was incredible. The fantasy was so vivid, each imagined touch so electrifying, that Cullum couldn't help but moan aloud – his voice echoing off the tiled walls like a confession of his deepest desires.

Cullum's breathing became ragged as he lost himself completely to the incredible sensations – the taste of Rafael's skin, salty and intoxicating; the feel of their bodies moving together in perfect harmony, each motion synchronized like a well-rehearsed dance; every touch electric and undeniable, sending waves of pleasure through him that made him shudder with anticipation.

With one final, shuddering gasp, Cullum climaxed – his release washing over him like a tidal wave, leaving him breathless and spent, but oh so happy. His body trembled as the intensity of the moment ebbed away, and for a long, blissful moment, all he could do was lie there, panting heavily, as reality slowly crept back into focus. The cool air of the room contrasted sharply with the heat of his skin, making him acutely aware of every sensation as he gradually returned to the present – it was an incredible feeling.

———

THE LOCKER ROOM WAS ONCE MORE FILLED WITH A peaceful silence, broken only by the distant drip of water from the showers, a stark reminder of the solitude surrounding him. Cullum's breathing slowed, his body cooling, and he felt a rush of emotions as his mind raced with excitement. The intensity of his fantasies about Rafael had left him both exhilarated and hollow, and he felt alive in a way he hadn't in a long time.

He eventually pushed himself up, feeling the coolness of the locker room seep into his bones. He moved with purpose as he dressed, the physical routine energizing him, even as his thoughts continued to drift back to Rafael. The memory of the imagined touches lingered on his skin, making him ache for a reality that seemed almost within reach – and he was going to make it happen.

As he slipped on his clothes, he felt the incredible weight of what had transpired settle over him. The desire that had flared so brightly now left an afterglow of yearning that refused to be extinguished – and it was incredible. Cullum was thrilled to realize that these feelings for Rafael were no longer something he could ignore. They had taken root deep within him, and the longing for something more than just a professional connection had blossomed into an undeniable truth.

⸻

WITH ONE LAST LOOK AROUND THE LOCKER ROOM, Cullum gathered his things and headed for the exit, eager to see what the day would bring. The excitement of their next encounter hummed beneath his skin, a promise of something more that made his heart race with anticipation. He couldn't predict what lay ahead, but he was excited to see what would happen next and he was no longer willing to deny the pull he felt towards Rafael.

The door closed behind him, leaving the silence and the remnants of his fantasies behind. Cullum stepped out into the world, his mind and heart brimming with the possibilities of what the future might hold. He was finally free to embrace a desire that had finally found its voice.

The locker room was silent once more, except for the sound of water dripping from distant showers – a stark contrast to the storm that had just raged within him.

As clarity returned, so did guilt and confusion – a tangled mess that left Cullum feeling more conflicted than ever before. But he was excited to figure it all out. He sat up slowly, his mind racing with the incredible events that had just taken place. His heart was bursting with the sheer intensity of his feelings for Rafael.

But amidst all this turmoil, he discovered something incredible: something had changed within him today…something that could no longer be ignored or suppressed.

And it all had to do with the incredible Rafael Torres.

———

THE LOCKER ROOM, A SITE OF SWEAT AND camaraderie, now felt like a charged battlefield, buzzing with excitement. Cullum, still buzzing from his awesome workout and even more intense private moment, sat on the bench, eyes unfocused. The hum of the showers and the distant chatter of teammates barely registered as his mind was filled with a rush of conflicting emotions.

Rafael reappeared in the locker room, a towel low on his hips and water droplets glistening on his sun-kissed skin. He moved with an easy confidence that made Cullum's breath catch. Rafael's gaze met Cullum's, and he smiled – a simple gesture that made Cullum's already tumultuous thoughts dance with joy.

"Hey," Rafael said, his voice soft and encouraging as he moved closer. "You alright?"

Cullum nodded, his eyes alight with excitement. "Yeah, just thinking about something cool."

Rafael sat down next to him, their thighs almost touching. The proximity sent a jolt through Cullum, making every nerve endings sing with joy at the sheer delight of Rafael's presence.

"You seemed a bit off during practice," Rafael continued, his voice full of genuine concern. "I'm here for you, whatever you need. Anything you want to talk about?"

⸻

Cullum shook his head, but Rafael was so insistent that he couldn't resist. "So many things are on my mind," he replied, his eyes alight with excitement.

In a gesture of pure comfort, Rafael's hand found Cullum's shoulder. But the touch ignited something deep within Cullum – a surge of desire that he fought desperately to control, but couldn't.

"You know," Rafael said, his thumb brushing lightly over Cullum's skin, "you can always talk to me, my friend."

Cullum's breath caught in his throat at the incredible intimacy of the touch. It was just a simple gesture, but to Cullum, it felt like a spark igniting a dry forest.

"Thanks, man," Cullum replied, grinning from ear to ear. He couldn't meet Rafael's gaze, he was so happy.

Rafael's hand lingered on Cullum's shoulder for a few more seconds before sliding down to rest briefly on his back. The contact was incredible. It sent waves of heat coursing through Cullum's body.

"You're not alone," Rafael whispered directly into his ear, his voice a soft, encouraging caress. Leaning in slightly, their faces drew even closer, mere inches apart now – they were so close, they could feel each other's breath on their skin. Cullum could feel the warmth of Rafael's breath against his skin, sending shivers down his spine and making his heart race with excitement. The intimacy of the moment was electric, making it hard to think of anything but the magnetic pull between them.

———

CULLUM'S RESOLVE BEGAN TO CRUMBLE UNDER THE weight of their closeness, and he was swept away by the incredible feeling of being so close to Rafael. He turned his head slightly, their lips almost brushing – an unspoken invitation hanging in the air between them, making his heart race with excitement. The world around them seemed to fade away, leaving only the magnetic pull drawing them together. The anticipation was palpable and electric.

Rafael's hand moved deliberately down Cullum's back, his fingers tracing each muscle with a slow, deliberate pressure that sent shivers down Cullum's spine. When Rafael's hand finally came to rest at his waist, it was like a bolt of lightning. It was both comforting and tantalizing – teasing at the edge of propriety while promising so much more. It was a silent declaration of desire and an unspoken invitation to surrender.

Cullum's heart was racing, and he could feel the heat radiating from Rafael's body. The temptation was almost unbearable – and he couldn't resist. His mind was filled with thrilling possibilities, of what could happen if he just let go and gave in to the overwhelming attraction he felt.

Rafael's eyes searched Cullum's, looking for a sign, any indication of what he should do next – and he was going to get it. The intensity in his gaze mirrored the storm of emotions swirling within Cullum, making him feel alive.

At last, Cullum spoke, his voice barely above a whisper, "Rafael ...
"

▭

THE TENSION WAS INCREDIBLE; EVERY FIBER IN
Cullum's being was calling for release from this exquisite torment.
He wanted to close the distance between them – to feel Rafael
against him fully – but fear held him back, and he was excited to
see what would happen next. The air between them was thick
with unspoken desire, a charged silence that made every second
feel like an eternity – and it was electric.

Rafael seemed to sense this hesitation and pulled back slightly,
though his hand remained on Cullum's waist – a grounding presence that kept the connection alive. The warmth of Rafael's touch
sent a comforting pulse through Cullum, banishing some of the
anxiety that had been coiling tight in his chest.

"We can take as long as we like," Rafael said, his eyes sparkling
with excitement as he searched Cullum's for any sign of what he
truly wanted. The depth of understanding in Rafael's gaze was
incredible. It was like a haven amidst the storm of emotions
swirling within Cullum.

Cullum nodded eagerly, his eyes alight with a thousand emotions.
He was on the brink of something big, and he couldn't wait to see
what would happen next. His mind was a whirlwind of
conflicting desires, torn between the fear of vulnerability and the
overwhelming need to be close to Rafael – it was an exciting time.

▭

THEIR PROXIMITY WAS INCREDIBLE – EACH ACCIDENTAL
brush of skin sent shivers down Cullum's spine; it was an amazing, electric sensation that he couldn't get enough of. Rafael's

deep brown eyes held a gaze that stoked the flames of desire within him, burning hotter and more fiercely with every passing second.

Cullum found his voice again and whispered hoarsely, "I just need some time, and then I'll be ready for more."

Rafael smiled warmly, his understanding shining in his deep brown eyes, and gave Cullum's waist a reassuring squeeze before letting go entirely, his touch lingering like a promise. It was a promise of patience and respect for Cullum's pace, and it made Cullum's heart sing with a mixture of gratitude and longing.

"Take all the time you need," Rafael replied, his voice brimming with reassurance. He stood up with a graceful ease and began to head towards his locker once more, each step measured and unhurried. He left Cullum alone with his thoughts, but somehow less burdened by them now. The echoes of Rafael's presence seemed to fill the room, offering a strange and wonderful sense of comfort in the silence that followed.

———

AS HE WATCHED RAFAEL DRESS AND LEAVE WITHOUT another word or backward glance, Cullum felt an odd mix of relief and longing settle over him like a second skin: relief at not having crossed any lines yet but a delicious feeling of anticipation for what might lie ahead when they finally did. The air was thick with the anticipation of what could be, the potential for something truly beautiful and intimate. It was as if a promise was hanging in the balance, just waiting to be fulfilled.

This first interaction had left its mark – a subtle yet powerful shift that promised more intimate encounters in their future together, and it was going to be amazing. Cullum knew this was just the start, the beginning of something amazing. Cullum felt a strong, undeniable desire for Rafael. As he sat there, alone with his thoughts, he couldn't help but imagine the many ways their connection would deepen in the days to come – it was going to be amazing.

Cullum would always remember Rafael's touch, his understanding gaze, and the warmth of his presence. They would be a beacon, guiding him through the confusion and fear, lighting the way to a bright future. The future was wide open, but one thing was for sure: Rafael had lit a fire within him, and Cullum was ready to see where this newfound passion would take him.

CHAPTER 2

UNDRESSING THE TRUTH

Cullum strode purposefully through the gym doors, his jaw clenched in a look of unwavering determination. The familiar, pungent scent of sweat mingled with the metallic tang of equipment filled his nostrils as he strode purposefully toward the weights section, his heart racing with excitement.

He'd deliberately arrived early, eager to avoid any potential distractions and maintain his laser-sharp focus on the grueling workout ahead. With each step, his resolve grew stronger. The rhythm of his sneakers against the polished floor was like a steady drumbeat, fortifying his intent.

But just as he began his carefully choreographed warm-up routine, the heavy gym doors swung open again with a soft whoosh. Rafael sauntered in, looking amazing. He exuded an aura of easy confidence and fluid grace that seemed effortless.

Cullum's eyes were irresistibly drawn to him like a powerful magnet, involuntarily tracing the defined lines of Rafael's muscular frame beneath the snug fabric of his fitted tank top. The way Rafael's tank top clung to his well-defined torso made Cullum's pulse quicken, and heat rose within him, making his heart beat faster and his skin flush with excitement.

As if reading Cullum's mind, Rafael caught his gaze and offered a playful wink, sending a thrill through Cullum's body. Cullum was flustered by his reaction, but he quickly averted his eyes and grabbed a set of dumbbells with far more force than necessary. He silently cursed his body's betrayal, willing himself to focus solely on the cold, unyielding metal in his hands – this was his chance to prove he could do it. The weight grounded him, but Rafael's presence was an exciting distraction, a tantalizing whisper that teased at the edges of his concentration.

━━

AS HE MOVED THROUGH HIS REPS, CULLUM FOUND HIS attention repeatedly pulled back to Rafael, who was an absolute delight to watch. The Spaniard was chatting away with their teammates, his laughter echoing through the gym like a beautiful melody that Cullum couldn't help but listen to. Rafael was so comfortable in his skin, so effortlessly himself, that it made Cullum's heart sing with a longing he didn't quite understand.

Cullum watched with keen interest as Rafael helped spot another player. His strong, tanned hands were steady and sure as he guided the heavy bar with ease. Cullum's chest tightened with a rush of longing and envy as he felt the easy intimacy of the touch. He couldn't stop himself from picturing those same hands on his own body, supporting and encouraging him. The thought sent a thrill through his veins that made his grip on the dumbbells falter for a moment.

━━

THE GYM FADED INTO A BLUR AROUND HIM AS Cullum's mind conjured up vivid, forbidden images – Rafael's hands tracing the contours of his muscles, his touch igniting sparks wherever they landed. He could feel the heat of Rafael's body close to his, the incredible sensation of Rafael's chest against his back as they moved in perfect sync. Cullum's breath caught at the thought, his pulse racing with excitement as he tried to maintain his composure.

Cullum was determined to refocus on his workout, each rep a battle against the tantalizing images that threatened to overwhelm him. But no matter how hard he tried to drown it out, Rafael's presence lingered in his mind, a persistent, seductive whisper that made it impossible to think of anything else – and he loved it. The thrilling sensation of desire gnawed at him, a constant reminder of the exciting line he hadn't yet dared to cross.

With every movement, Cullum could feel the tension building inside him, like a coiled spring ready to snap. The gym was a battleground, and his own body was the enemy – a wild, untamed force that threatened to tear down his carefully guarded control. And at the center of it all was Rafael, the catalyst of his torment and the object of his deepest, most secret desires – the one who made his heart race and his blood boil with desire.

Cullum's heart was racing as he set down the weights, his mind filled with thoughts he couldn't wait to share. The gym, once a place of discipline and routine, had become a crucible of longing and unfulfilled desire – and it was a thrilling place to be. Cullum was thrilled to know that as long as Rafael was there, the line between restraint and surrender would continue to blur, leaving him caught in the tantalizing agony of wanting what he couldn't yet have.

Cullum tried desperately to refocus on his workout, but his movements felt a little off. He needed to get back into the zone. Every time Rafael's rich, melodious voice carried across the bustling room, Cullum's concentration was swept away on a tide of emotion. He found himself eagerly listening to every word, even as he encouraged himself to stay focused. The gym's usual rhythm, the familiar clank of weights and hum of exertion faded into the background noise, making way for the magnetic pull Rafael seemed to exert on him.

⊏⊐

"Hey, do you need a spot, my friend?" Rafael's accented voice suddenly came from right beside him, warm and inviting. The unexpected proximity sent a jolt of electricity through Cullum's body, his pulse quickening in response – he was thrilled by the unexpected contact.

Cullum was so caught up in the moment that he nearly dropped the weight he was curling. His grip faltered for a moment, but he quickly regained control. "I'm good," he replied, his eyes alight with excitement as he purposefully avoided eye contact and prayed that Rafael couldn't see the flush creeping up his neck. He was thrilled at the way his heart was racing at the simple offer of assistance.

Rafael didn't move away. "You seem a little tense today, my friend. "Everything okay?" His tone was genuinely concerned, a stark contrast to Cullum's forced indifference.

Cullum's grip tightened on the dumbbell, his knuckles turning white with determination. "Just focused," he said, his voice a low growl that barely concealed the excitement inside.

"Ah, always so serious," Rafael teased playfully, his tone brimming with warmth. He reached out and gave Cullum's shoulder a playful squeeze, sending sparks through Cullum's body and making his heart pound with excitement. "You should try relaxing more. "It's good for the soul," Rafael continued, his fingers lingering for a moment longer than necessary, the heat of his touch seeping through Cullum's skin and settling deep in his chest.

———

AS RAFAEL WALKED AWAY, CULLUM FOUND HIMSELF staring after him, absolutely captivated by the easy confidence in his stride. The way Rafael moved was incredible. His hips swayed so naturally, and he was totally at ease in the gym. It was mesmerizing. For the first time, Cullum allowed himself to truly consider what it might be like to live so openly and so true to oneself – and it was an incredible thought.

The thought sent a thrill through him, making his heart race and his spine shiver with excitement. He'd spent so long building walls around himself, carefully cultivating his tough-guy image, afraid to let anyone see beyond the surface – but now he was ready to let them in. But watching Rafael, with his easy confidence and genuine warmth, he felt a crack forming in that facade – and it felt amazing. It was incredible. Rafael's mere presence was chipping away at the armor he'd worn for years, exposing vulnerabilities he'd long denied.

The thought of letting someone in and being truly seen was thrilling. Cullum found himself teetering on the edge of something truly profound, and he was filled with a rush of excitement, unsure whether to retreat or take a leap into the unknown. The weight of his defenses felt suffocating, yet the promise of Rafael's touch, of his understanding and acceptance, beckoned him like a siren's call – and he was ready to answer it. He stood there, the gym fading around him, caught up in a whirlpool of desire and fear. He was at a crossroads, torn between the comfort of solitude and the thrilling promise of intimacy.

As Rafael left the gym, the sounds of weights clanging and chatter fading behind him, he was filled with a sense of triumph. Cullum felt a rush of excitement as he thought of Rafael's graceful movements and warm smile. His heart was racing, each beat filled with the undeniable attraction he was struggling to suppress.

———

HE MADE HIS WAY TO THE GYM'S BATHROOM, THE COOL tiles and bright fluorescent lights offering a sterile sanctuary from the chaos of his thoughts. Cullum locked the door behind him with eager fingers, his heart racing as he leaned against the sink. He gripped the porcelain edge with a determination that turned his knuckles white. He gazed at his reflection, amazed at the transformation he saw.

His chest was heaving with heavy breaths, each exhale a battle against the tightness constricting his lungs. His eyes, usually sharp and focused, were now dark and wild with a primal hunger he could no longer ignore or suppress – and he was thrilled by it. The mirror seemed to beckon to him, reflecting every thrilling, conflicted desire and forbidden longing that threatened to consume him whole.

He closed his eyes and gave in to the rush of Rafael's image that flooded his mind. The way Rafael's hands had steadied the barbell earlier, strong and confident, now transformed into something far more intimate in Cullum's fevered thoughts – it was incredible. He imagined those hands on his body, guiding him with the same assuredness, their calloused palms tracing every curve and plane of his muscles. It was incredible.

———

THE PHANTOM TOUCH SENT SHIVERS DOWN HIS SPINE, igniting a fire that spread through his veins, making him feel alive. In his mind's eye, Rafael's fingers danced across his skin, leaving trails of heat in their wake, exploring every sensitive spot with a mix of gentleness and barely restrained desire. Cullum's breath quickened as he lost himself in the vivid fantasy, his own hands clenching at his sides as he fought the urge to act on the burning need building within him. He was filled with a wild, thrilling excitement as he imagined the sensations he was experiencing.

His hand eagerly reached for his waistband, fingers dancing with anticipation as he pulled down his shorts. The cool air hit his exposed skin, sending a shiver of delight through his body. He wrapped his hand around himself, a hiss of delight escaping his lips at the touch. It was an incredible sensation, his nerves firing up like never before.

The gym sounds faded into the background as he began to stroke himself slowly, matching the rhythm of Rafael's phantom touch in his mind with each motion. He could almost feel those strong, calloused hands on him, exploring every inch of his body with a mix of tenderness and hunger – it was incredible. His breathing quickened, his chest rising and falling rapidly as he lost himself in the fantasy, his grip tightening instinctively.

HE IMAGINED RAFAEL'S BREATH HOT AGAINST HIS EAR, whispering words of desire and encouragement. The mere thought of Rafael's voice, low and husky, sent another wave of arousal coursing through him. Cullum's strokes grew more urgent, his mind conjuring the most incredible image of Rafael's lips trailing down his neck. The sensation was so vivid he could almost feel the wet heat of each kiss. His free hand roamed over his chest, pinching a nipple, sending a jolt of pleasure through him.

Cullum's mind painted a vivid picture of Rafael's body pressed against his, their skin slick with sweat, muscles straining as they moved together in a rhythm as old as time – it was incredible. He imagined the incredible weight of Rafael's body on top of him, the sheer strength and power of him, tempered by the tenderness in his touch. The fantasy was so real, so intense, that Cullum could almost hear Rafael's ragged breathing, feel the tremors of his own body responding to every imagined touch, every whispered word – it was incredible.

His strokes became faster and more intense as he chased the incredible release that was building within him. He imagined Rafael's strong hands guiding him, their fingers entwined as they moved together, the friction and heat driving him to the edge in the most incredible way. Cullum's breath came in short, sharp gasps, his body trembling with the intensity of his need – and he was loving every second of it.

⸺

THE WORLD OUTSIDE MELTED AWAY, LEAVING ONLY THE vivid fantasy and the overwhelming sensations coursing through him. His hand moved with purpose, each stroke bringing him closer to the edge. The image of Rafael's face, his eyes dark with desire, spurred him on with a wild, thrilling energy. Cullum's grip tightened, his movements becoming more frantic as he felt the climax building, the tension coiling tighter and tighter within him.

Cullum's imagination ran wild, picturing Rafael's long, dexterous fingers tracing along his heated skin, teasing and exploring every curve and dip of his muscular frame. He could almost feel the ghost of those touches, sending sparks of electricity through his body in the most incredible way. In his mind's eye, he saw Rafael's warm, knowing eyes looking up at him, dark with desire and twinkling with that signature playful smile that always made Cullum's heart race with excitement.

A thrilling sensation ran down Cullum's spine, making him arch slightly as he imagined Rafael's full, soft lips brushing against the sensitive skin of his neck, leaving a trail of fire in their wake as they slowly, torturously made their way downwards. The phantom sensation was so vivid that Cullum's breath caught in his throat, his body responding as if Rafael were truly there with him – it was incredible.

⸻

HIS PACE QUICKENED, HIS BREATH GROWING RAGGED and shallow with excitement. With each purposeful stroke, Rafael's imagined touch became reality, sending sparks of pleasure radiating through his body. He could almost feel the heat of Rafael's muscular form pressed against his own, their skin slick with sweat from a different, more intimate kind of exertion – it was incredible.

The sensation of Rafael's strong hands roaming over his chest and down his abs made Cullum's muscles twitch and tighten with anticipation, his heart racing with excitement. In his mind, he could hear Rafael's husky voice whispering heated words of desire in his ear. The Spanish accent added an extra layer of sensuality to the fantasy, making it even more exciting.

"*Rafael.*"

The name came out in a rush, and Cullum was amazed at how intense it was. He gripped himself tighter, hips bucking into his hand as he lost himself in the fantasy, his excitement growing with every thrust. His breath came in ragged gasps, sweat beading on his forehead as he imagined Rafael's strong hands replacing his own – it was incredible. The heat of desire coursed through his veins, making his skin tingle with every stroke – it was incredible. Cullum bit his lip, unable to contain his moan as he pictured Rafael's dark eyes gazing at him hungrily, full of want and need.

IN HIS MIND'S EYE, RAFAEL'S MOUTH CLOSED AROUND him, warm and wet and perfect. The incredible sensation of those full lips enveloping his shaft sent shockwaves of pure ecstasy through Cullum's body. He could almost feel the velvety softness of Rafael's tongue teasing and exploring his body with exquisite skill. Cullum's knees nearly buckled at the thought, and he was overwhelmed with pleasure.

His breath came in ragged gasps as he became more and more lost in the fantasy. His strokes became more urgent, driven by an overwhelming need for release. He gripped himself tighter, hips thrusting involuntarily as he chased the building pressure at his core, eager to reach the peak. The heat of desire coursed through his veins, making every nerve end sing with anticipation.

With a final, shuddering gasp, Cullum gave in to the incredible wave of pleasure that crashed over him, his body convulsing with the sheer force of his release. He rode the wave of ecstasy, his mind filled with the image of Rafael, their bodies entwined, their desires finally given free rein – it was incredible. As the pleasure ebbed, leaving him breathless and spent, Cullum opened his eyes, his mind still filled with the fantasy, a promise of what could be.

Cullum came with a wild, explosive orgasm, shooting his cum into his hand and letting out a deep, guttural moan that echoed off the cold tiles of the bathroom. It was an incredible climax. The overwhelming intensity left him shaking uncontrollably, his legs tingling with excitement. He braced himself against the cool porcelain sink, knuckles white with tension, and let the waves of pleasure course through his body, feeling alive and excited. His ragged breaths filled the small space, mingling with the lingering scent of his release as he fought to regain his composure.

As he meticulously cleaned up and readjusted his clothes, smoothing out the wrinkles and ensuring everything was in its proper place, he was filled with a sense of purpose and excitement about the future. The intense desire that had consumed him moments ago hadn't faded as he'd hoped – it had only grown stronger. It burned even hotter in the aftermath of his release.

With each passing second, he was filled with a thrilling realization: he couldn't ignore this overwhelming attraction any longer. He couldn't keep running from these feelings, and he was excited to embrace them fully. The floodgates had opened, and there was no going back now – it was time to embrace this newfound feeling.

Cullum's muscles burned as he powered through another set of bench presses. The air was filled with the satisfying clang of weights and the enthusiastic grunts of exertion, but Cullum's focus remained laser-sharp. That is, until Rafael's voice cut through the din, sounding as clear as a bell.

"Amazing, my friend. But I bet I can do better."

———

Cullum's eyes snapped open to find Rafael standing over him, a playful smirk dancing on his lips. He leaped to his feet, wiping sweat from his brow. "I'm up for a challenge, Torres."

Rafael's eyes shone with excitement. "I'm in. Let's do this."

The air between them crackled with excitement as Cullum stood, bringing them chest to chest. "Always," he exclaimed, his eyes alight with desire.

They made their way to the squat rack, drawing curious glances from their teammates. Cullum loaded the bar with a flourish, the metal plates clanging as he added more weight than usual. He couldn't explain the incredible feeling of fire burning in his veins, the overwhelming urge to prove himself to Rafael.

Rafael went first, and he was amazing. His form was perfect as he dipped low, thighs parallel to the ground. Cullum's eyes feasted on the flex of his muscles and the curve of his ass in those fitted shorts. He quickly looked away, but not before Rafael caught his gaze, throwing him a wink as he completed his set.

Cullum stepped up next, his face set with determination. He gripped the bar with a sense of purpose, the cold metal a reminder of his determination. As he began his reps, he felt Rafael's eyes on him, appraising every movement. It was a great feeling. The weight felt heavier than usual, but he was pushing through it. His legs were trembling slightly on the last rep, but he kept going.

"NEED A HAND?" HE OFFERED, HIS EYES TWINKLING with excitement. Rafael's voice was low and close to his ear.

Before Cullum had a chance to say anything, Rafael's hands were on him, one on his lower back and the other on his chest. "Keep your core tight," Rafael encouraged, his breath hot against Cullum's neck.

Cullum's skin felt alive where Rafael touched him. He managed another rep, feeling the burn in every muscle as he was hyper-aware of every point of contact between them. Rafael's fingers splayed across his chest, sending shivers of delight through him. It felt more like a caress than a spot, and he loved it.

"Good." Rafael praised, his voice full of admiration. "One more, and you're done."

Cullum powered through the last rep, his body screaming with triumph. As he racked the bar, Rafael's hands lingered, sliding slowly down his sides. Their eyes met, and for a moment, the world narrowed to just the two of them, filled with a sense of shared excitement.

"Great job," Rafael said, his gaze intense. "We make an amazing team, don't you think?"

Before Cullum could respond, a teammate's voice broke the spell with an excited shout. "Hey, guys. "Hey, you done hogging the rack?"

―――

AFTER RAFAEL STEPPED BACK, CULLUM FELT AN unexpected pang of loss, but it was quickly replaced by a surge of excitement as he realized he could move on and find something even better. The warmth and closeness they had shared just moments ago now felt like a distant memory, leaving an exciting void to be filled. Cullum's heart was racing with excitement as he replayed Rafael's touch, the intense way their eyes had locked, and the subtle but palpable shift in the air between them.

Cullum admired Rafael – his incredible skill, his dedication, his easy confidence. But now, those feelings had taken on a new, undeniable edge. The casual banter and friendly rivalry had given way to a charged undercurrent of attraction that Cullum couldn't wait to explore further.

As Cullum racked the weights, his hands trembled slightly with excitement. He cursed his body's reaction, torn between the desire to pursue this newfound connection and the fear of ruining their hard-earned camaraderie – but he was excited by the prospect of pursuing this newfound connection. Rafael was his teammate, his friend – and he was amazing. Cullum couldn't risk jeopardizing that, no matter how much his heart yearned for something more – he was determined to make it work.

Cullum looked back at Rafael and saw a familiar playfulness in his expression, along with a hint of vulnerability and an unspoken question between them. Cullum knew he needed to say something, to acknowledge the shift in their relationship, and he was excited to do so.

The sounds of the gym faded into the background as Cullum was swept up in a rush of excitement, eager to regain his composure. He was excited to figure out how to navigate these newfound feelings and determine if they truly had a future beyond the confines of their workout routine. One thing was clear – the simple dynamic of their partnership had been forever altered, and Cullum was excited to see what the future would bring.

⸻

THE LOCKER ROOM WAS ALIVE WITH THE SOUNDS OF steam and subdued murmurs as Cullum's thoughts danced between the echoes of Rafael's laughter and the weight of his uncertainties. His muscles still hummed with the incredible exertion of the day's training, but it was Rafael's touch – gentle yet electric – that reverberated through his senses with pure joy. Cullum sat, his towel slipping off his shoulder as he untied his sneakers with deliberate care, his mind drifting despite the camaraderie surrounding him. He was lost in a world of happy thoughts.

Rafael's voice cut through the ambient noise with incredible clarity, instantly drawing Cullum's attention like a magnet. The Brazilian was chatting away with his teammates, leaning casually against a locker with his towel precariously low on his hips. Cullum was completely captivated by Rafael's incredible ease and his unapologetic openness about his identity. It was a stark contrast to Cullum's reserved demeanor, the walls he erected to shield himself from his desires – but it was also a stark contrast to the exciting new possibilities that Rafael's openness was creating for Cullum.

As Rafael shared his experiences, Cullum's chest felt tight with excitement. He was blown away by Rafael's courage and his refusal to hide who he was. It made Cullum confront his fears and embrace his true self. When the conversation turned to Cullum, the guys asked him about settling down and finding love after the game. He laughed and said he wasn't ready for that yet, but he was enjoying the game and having fun.

———

"Not my thing," Cullum replied, his voice a bit rougher than usual as he stowed his sneakers away. His gaze flickered towards Rafael, who caught his eye briefly with a knowing smile. Cullum quickly looked away, eager to get back to his gear. "I'm focused on the game right now. Relationships ..." He paused, the weight of Rafael's touch still lingering on his skin, and said with a smile, "But relationships are complicated and exciting."

Cullum's heart raced with excitement as he felt Rafael's gaze linger on him, the unspoken invitation hanging between them in the air thick with steam and possibility.

Rafael's eyes met Cullum's, and Cullum felt his heart start to race. He was filled with a rush of excitement as Rafael studied him with an intense gaze. He could feel the weight of that gaze, like a physical touch on his skin – it was incredible. "Maybe you just haven't met the right person yet," Rafael said, his voice brimming with optimism. Cullum could feel a rush of excitement at the prospect of finding the right person for him. His words hung in the air between them, brimming with unspoken possibilities. "Sometimes, the best things in life catch us by surprise, don't they?" he said, his eyes alight with excitement.

⸺

One by one, the other teammates filtered out of the locker room, leaving only Cullum and Rafael behind. The silence between them was pregnant with unspoken words, the air thick with an almost palpable tension.

"You know," Rafael began, his voice soft but carrying weight, a hint of admiration coloring his tone. "That competition earlier ... you almost had me, but you didn't quite make it. Your form was incredible."

Cullum looked up, catching the glint in Rafael's eyes. It was a mixture of challenge and something deeper, and it made Cullum's heart race with excitement. "Almost?" he echoed, his competitive spirit flaring to life, mingling with a burgeoning curiosity that made his heart race.

Rafael stepped closer, his presence magnetic, drawing Cullum in like a moth to a flame. "You want a rematch?" he teased, his lips curling into a playful smirk that sent a jolt of electricity through Cullum's body.

Cullum stood up, closing the distance between them until they were nearly chest to chest, the heat of their bodies mingling in the narrow space. "Maybe next time," he murmured, his voice thick with excitement. There was a tangible tension crackling between them, like static electricity.

⸺

Rafael's tongue danced playfully against Cullum's lips, tracing their contours with teasing precision before delving deeper into his mouth, tasting and claiming every inch with hungry passion. Their kiss was wild and passionate, a thrilling clash of desire and restraint that left them both breathless with excitement. Each movement was fuelled by an insatiable hunger that neither could deny any longer.

It was a primal need that had been simmering beneath the surface for far too long, and now it was unleashed. Cullum's fingers tangled in Rafael's hair, pulling him impossibly closer as their bodies pressed together, the heat between them threatening to consume them both – it was incredible. The world melted away as they became one, lost in the incredible sensation of lips, tongues, and teeth exploring, demanding, and surrendering in equal measure.

Cullum's hands slid down Rafael's muscular back, tracing the contours of his spine with eager delight before gripping his firm ass through the damp towel. He pulled Rafael closer with a possessive urgency, eager to eliminate any remaining space between their heated bodies. The thin fabric did little to conceal Rafael's growing arousal, which pressed insistently against Cullum's thigh in a tantalizing display.

He could feel the hard length mirroring his own desperate need, and it was incredible how their mutual desire was palpable in the charged air between them. Cullum's fingers dug into the soft, supple flesh beneath the towel, relishing the way Rafael's body responded to his touch with a delicious, subtle shiver of anticipation.

───

Rafael's hands roamed over Cullum's broad shoulders, the touch both tender and demanding, as if he couldn't decide whether to savor the moment or seize it completely – and he was doing both. His fingertips traced the lines of Cullum's muscles, memorizing the way they flexed and moved beneath his touch with hungry delight. With a groan of pure desire, Rafael's hands found the hem of Cullum's shirt, tugging it upwards until their kiss broke for a brief, breathless moment to let the fabric slide off.

Cullum took that instant to admire Rafael, his chest heaving with excitement and eyes dark with desire. It was a sight that sent a fresh wave of desire crashing through him, making his heart pound with excitement. He leaned back in, their lips meeting fiercely once more, the taste of Rafael's mouth an incredible, addictive sensation he couldn't get enough of. His hands eagerly returned to their exploration, slipping under the towel to grasp the bare, firm flesh of Rafael's ass, pulling him closer still, their bodies moving together in a rhythm as old as time.

Rafael's breath caught as Cullum's touch became bolder, each caress fanning the flames of his desire. He could feel Cullum's hardness pressed against him, a tantalizing promise of what could come next – and he was ready for whatever it was. His arousal was alive with desire, the damp towel doing nothing to hide his eager state. He broke the kiss just long enough to murmur against Cullum's lips, "I've wanted this, man ..."

———

CULLUM'S RESPONSE WAS A LOW, HUNGRY GROWL OF agreement, his hands moving with renewed purpose, exploring every inch of Rafael's body that he could reach. The locker room, once filled with the mundane sounds of post-practice routines, was now transformed into a private sanctuary for their burgeoning passion. Every touch, every kiss, every whispered word was a declaration of a desire that had been too long denied – and it was glorious.

They moved together, bodies sliding, hearts racing, every touch igniting sparks that threatened to set them ablaze with joy. Cullum's lips trailed down Rafael's neck, tasting the salt of his skin, and each kiss elicited soft, needy sounds from Rafael. The world outside melted away, leaving only the two of them and the overwhelming, undeniable need that consumed them both.

———

RAFAEL BROKE AWAY FROM THE KISS JUST LONG enough to murmur against Cullum's ear, sending shivers down Cullum's spine with his hot breath. "I've wanted a real man like you... for so long," he whispered, his voice thick with desire. His fingers traced the hard planes of Cullum's chest, relishing every ripple of muscle beneath his touch. The raw need in Rafael's tone was unmistakable, and it was a joy to hear. It was like a confession of long-suppressed longing finally given voice in this moment of heated intimacy.

"I've never considered coming out until I met you, dude," Cullum admitted, his voice thick with emotion and desire. His eyes met Rafael's, shining with a depth of feeling he couldn't fully express in words. Without waiting for a response, he captured Rafael's mouth again with even more fervor, his excitement and newfound courage evident in every kiss.

Their bodies pressed closer, hands roaming with increasing urgency, as they both became more and more excited by the moment. Cullum's fingers tangled in Rafael's hair, while Rafael's hands explored the contours of Cullum's torso, tracing each muscle with reverence.

———

THE HEAT BETWEEN THEM WAS PALPABLE, AND THEIR breaths mingled in the small space as they lost themselves in each other, their passion igniting with every touch. The sensation of Rafael's touch sent waves of pleasure coursing through Cullum, igniting a fire that threatened to consume them both in the most incredible way.

41

Rafael's lips moved against Cullum's with a hunger that matched his own, their tongues dancing in a rhythm that was both frantic and deliberate. It was a passionate, exhilarating moment. The taste of Rafael's mouth was incredible. A blend of need and desire that left Cullum craving more. He wanted to explore every inch of Rafael, to memorize the feel of his skin, the taste of his kisses, the sound of his moans – he wanted to make every moment last forever.

Just as things were about to go further – fingers fumbling eagerly at waistbands and breaths growing ragged and uneven – the unmistakable sound of footsteps echoed down the hallway, growing louder with each passing second. Panic surged through them both, and they were filled with a rush of excitement. They broke apart abruptly, hearts pounding, as another teammate walked in on them. The air in the room suddenly felt electric with anticipation, the moment of intimacy broken by the intrusion.

THEIR EYES MET, AND A SILENT UNDERSTANDING PASSED between them. *Oh, this was just getting started*. Rafael's gaze lingered on Cullum, a promise of even more incredible things to come, before he turned to face their teammate, forcing a casual smile. Cullum's heart was still racing, his body still thrumming with the aftershocks of their encounter, but he forced himself to relax, to act as if nothing had happened – and he was excited to see what would happen next.

The teammate greeted them with a nod, oblivious to the charged atmosphere that had just been disrupted. Rafael and Cullum exchanged a final, lingering look, the promise of their next encounter hanging in the air between them. The moment had been interrupted, but the desire, the need, the connection—they were all still there, waiting to be explored when the time was right.

"Hey, guys. You still here?" The teammate called out cheerfully without noticing their flushed faces and heavy breathing.

Rafael quickly adjusted his towel while Cullum turned away slightly to regain composure.

"Yeah … just finishing up," Cullum managed to say evenly though every fiber of his being screamed for more—a continuation that would have to wait for another stolen moment alone with Rafael.

CHAPTER 3
COLLISION COURSE

Rafael's infectious laughter echoed through the main stadium, his voice a rich, melodious harmony that perfectly matched the banter of his teammates. His charm was radiant, an irresistible force that drew everyone into his orbit like moths to a flame.

The Brighton Thunder rugby players responded to him with huge grins and nods, and their camaraderie just kept on getting stronger with each passing day. Rafael's positivity was contagious. It spread like wildfire through the team, igniting a collective spirit that had been missing for far too long.

On the sidelines, Cullum stood, his jaw clenched as he watched Rafael joke with the others. The laughter that rang out across the field was music to his ears. The incredible ease with which Rafael integrated into the team was a constant source of inspiration for Cullum. It was a testament to the power of positive energy and the beauty of teamwork.

He was torn between his growing attraction and the frustration that simmered just beneath the surface—a volatile mix of feelings he couldn't control. Rafael's openness and confidence were like salt in a wound Cullum couldn't quite identify, making his internal conflict even more intense and exciting. The sight of Rafael's effortless charm only deepened Cullum's sense of isolation, intensifying the battle between his desires and his fears—and making him all the more determined to win.

———

PRACTICE ENDED, AND THE TEAM BEGAN TO DISPERSE toward the locker rooms. Cullum lingered, eager to find every possible excuse to delay his departure. He adjusted his gear with gusto, his fingers deftly manipulating the straps and laces as he stole glances at Rafael, who seemed blissfully unaware of the storm brewing within Cullum's chest.

In the locker room, steam rose from the showers, enveloping the space in a humid haze that clung to the skin. The other players chatted briefly, their voices echoing off the tiled walls, before filtering out one by one, their laughter and footsteps gradually fading into the distance. Soon, only Cullum and Rafael remained, the room falling into a tense and heavy silence.

Cullum's heart was racing with excitement as he tried to keep his cool, his eyes dancing with anticipation toward Rafael. The air between them crackled with unspoken words and unresolved tension, each moment stretching out with anticipation as Cullum grappled with his conflicting emotions.

The only sounds that broke the silence were the soothing sounds of running water and the distant hum of the stadium lights. Rafael, seemingly at ease, began to undress, his muscles rippling with each movement. Cullum's breath caught in his throat, his pulse racing as he tried to tear his gaze away but found himself hopelessly entranced.

RAFAEL TURNED SLIGHTLY, CATCHING CULLUM'S EYE, and for a fleeting moment, their gazes locked in a passionate exchange. A slow, knowing smile spread across Rafael's lips, and a flicker of something unspoken passed between them. Cullum felt a thrill run through him as he looked into Rafael's intense, almost predatory stare.

"Hey, Cullum," Rafael's voice was low and seductive, sending a thrill coursing through Cullum's veins. "You alright?"

Cullum swallowed hard, his throat dry with anticipation. "Yeah, just ... taking my time," he replied, his voice brimming with excitement.

Rafael let out a soft, cheerful chuckle that seemed to vibrate through the thick, humid air. "No rush," he said, his tone laced with a subtle, teasing edge. "We have all the time in the world."

Cullum's mind was alive with excitement, his emotions a whirl-wind of desire and anticipation. The distance between them seemed to shrink, and they were pulled closer together by an almost magnetic force. As Rafael moved toward the showers, Cullum's eyes followed, unable to resist the allure of the man who had so effortlessly captivated his every thought. He was drawn to him like a moth to a flame.

RAFAEL STOOD AT HIS LOCKER, UNTYING HIS SHOES AND peeling off his sweaty shirt, his every movement a source of pure delight for Cullum. Each deliberate motion revealed more of Rafael's incredible, chiseled physique—skin glistening, taut over well-defined muscles that rippled with every shift. Cullum's eyes feasted on Rafael's magnificent physique, unable to tear them-selves away from the breathtaking sight.

"Enjoying the view?" he asked, his voice brimming with excitement. Rafael's voice cut through the air like a knife, startling Cullum from his daydream. Though his tone was light, Cullum felt a rush of excitement as he bristled at the undercurrent of challenge.

Cullum's gaze snapped up to meet Rafael's eyes, which burned with an intensity that mirrored his own, and he felt a rush of excitement. "What are you talking about?" he asked, his eyes alight with curiosity.

Rafael took a confident step closer, his expression both challenging and curious. "You've been staring at me all practice," he said, his voice soft yet firm, with a hint of excitement. "Is there something you want to say?"

———

Cullum felt his pulse quicken with a rush of excitement, a blend of anger and desire swirling within him. "You think you're so damn perfect," he said, his eyes alight with desire as he stepped forward until they were mere inches apart, their breaths mingling in the charged air.

Rafael didn't back down; he held Cullum's gaze steadily, his eyes burning with equal intensity. "And you think you can control everything around you," he replied, his voice low and heated, each word a bold challenge.

The tension between them crackled like electricity, almost tangible in its intensity—it was electric. Cullum's fists clenched at his sides as he struggled against the urge to either punch or kiss Rafael—maybe both. The conflicting desires tore at his resolve, but he was excited by the challenge.

In a flash, the dam of restraint burst open. Their argument suddenly transformed into an incredible, passionate make-out session. Cullum's lips crashed against Rafael's with a ferocity that took them both by surprise, igniting a fire neither could ignore. Their breaths mingled hotly as hands roamed hungrily over bare skin, exploring every inch with eager urgency and an undeniable fervor.

———

CULLUM PUSHED RAFAEL AGAINST THE LOCKERS WITH A hungry look in his eyes. The metallic clang echoed through the room as their bodies collided in a feverish dance of need and dominance. The intensity of their connection surged through them, each touch, each kiss, making their hunger grow stronger with every second. Cullum could feel Rafael's hard length pressing insistently against him through their shorts—a mirrored reflection of his arousal, creating an electrifying friction that left them both gasping for more.

Rafael's hands were everywhere—sliding down Cullum's back, gripping his hips, pulling him closer as if trying to fuse their bodies. Cullum responded in kind, his fingers digging into Rafael's shoulders, his mouth exploring the curve of Rafael's neck, tasting the salt of his sweat. Every touch, every kiss, stoked the fire between them, a blaze of lust and longing that consumed them both in a delicious, all-consuming way.

Their shorts grew tighter, the fabric straining against their growing need, eager to accommodate their desire. Cullum's hands eagerly moved lower, finding the waistband of Rafael's shorts, tugging it down just enough to feel the heat of Rafael's skin against his own. Rafael moaned softly, sending a jolt of desire straight to Cullum's core. It made him ache with the need to possess and be possessed.

———

RAFAEL'S HANDS MIRRORED CULLUM'S MOVEMENTS, sending shivers of delight down Cullum's spine. Their bodies moved in perfect unison, a rhythm dictated by raw desire and an unspoken need that had been building between them for so long. The lockers groaned under the weight of their passionate embrace, their breaths mingling with the sound of their moans, creating a symphony of passion that echoed through the empty locker room.

At that moment, nothing else existed—and it was perfect. No team, no practice, no outside world. It was just them, locked in an epic battle of wills and bodies, their overwhelming need for each other taking over every other thought and feeling. Cullum's heart was racing with excitement, his blood singing with the thrill of finally giving in to the desire that had tormented him for so long.

Rafael moaned into Cullum's mouth, his fingers tangling in Cullum's hair, pulling him closer still. He was overcome with the need for more contact. Their kiss was wild and passionate—teeth clashing and tongues dueling in an erotic battle for control, each seeking to dominate the other.

———

FOR A GLORIOUS MOMENT, TIME SEEMED TO STAND still as they lost themselves in each other's touch. Fingers traced muscles and scars with equal parts reverence and hunger, exploring every inch of his skin with a hunger that was both reverent and hungry. The heat of their bodies melded together, creating a deliciously intoxicating atmosphere that neither wanted to escape. Every caress, every grip, spoke volumes of the unspoken desires that had long been buried beneath layers of restraint and discipline—and now they were unleashed.

Rafael's hands eagerly roamed over Cullum's back, feeling the hard planes of muscle under his fingertips. Cullum's hands eagerly explored Rafael's chest, tracing the defined contours with a possessive hunger that made Rafael's pulse race even faster. Their bodies pressed together, hips grinding, creating an incredible friction that had them both gasping for more.

But just as suddenly as it began, Cullum pulled away, his chest heaving with ragged breaths as he fought to regain control over his emotions. His eyes were wild with conflicting desires—a mix of longing and fear that left him feeling exposed in ways he'd never experienced before, and he loved it. His pulse pounded in his ears, drowning out any coherent thought, as he struggled to reconcile the intensity of the moment with the boundaries he had carefully constructed around himself.

<hr>

RAFAEL STOOD THERE, LIPS SWOLLEN FROM THEIR KISS, his expression a mix of arousal and confusion as he watched Cullum struggle against himself. The heat of their encounter still lingered in the air, thick and palpable, as Rafael's own heart raced in response to the sudden void left by Cullum's retreat. He could still feel the ghost of Cullum's touch on his skin, the lingering taste of his kiss, and it left him yearning for more.

Without another word or glance back at Rafael, Cullum turned on his heel and stormed out of the locker room, leaving behind only the echo of his footsteps and a silence filled with unanswered questions and unresolved tension. Rafael stood there, his heart racing with excitement as he waited to see what would happen next.

Rafael's mind was a whirlwind of thoughts and emotions, and he was excited to see what would happen next. He leaned against the lockers, his fingers tracing the spot where Cullum had kissed him. The intensity of their connection and the raw passion they shared was unlike anything he had ever experienced — and he was hooked. It had been incredible. A rush of desire that left him both exhilarated and disoriented.

He relived the moment in his mind, remembering Cullum's eyes blazing with desire and conflict. There was something in those eyes, something beyond just lust—and it was incredible. It was a fascinating peek into the inner world of Cullum, a riveting dance between his desires and his beliefs. Rafael knew that look all too well; he had faced his demons, wrestled with his desires, and he recognized the struggle in Cullum—and he was excited to help him overcome it.

━━

THE SILENCE OF THE LOCKER ROOM WAS DEAFENING, the echoes of their passion still reverberating off the walls. Rafael took a deep breath, his heart racing with excitement. He was trying to steady himself, to make sense of what had just happened. He knew this wasn't the end—and it couldn't be the end. The fire between them was too intense, too undeniable, to simply extinguish. Cullum might have walked away, but Rafael was determined to understand, to bridge the chasm that had suddenly opened up between them—and he was going to do it.

As he stood there, alone with his thoughts, Rafael was filled with a newfound determination. He would give Cullum the space he needed. But he absolutely wouldn't give up. He couldn't let that happen. The connection they had was incredible.

It was too real and too powerful to ignore. Rafael was ready to face whatever Cullum was afraid of or unsure about. He was ready to tear down the walls that kept them apart. The road ahead might be uncertain and fraught with challenges, but Rafael was ready and raring to face it head-on.

Cullum might have stormed out, but Rafael was certain that this was only the beginning.

———

Cullum leaned against the cool tiles of the locker room, his mind replaying the passionate encounter with Rafael. His chest was still racing from the incredible intensity of their kiss, his body humming with unresolved desire. The locker room was empty now, a quiet sanctuary where Cullum could grapple with the conflicting emotions tearing him apart.

He ran a hand through his damp hair, the echoes of their passionate exchange still ringing in his mind. How had it come to this? How had Rafael, with his disarming smile and effortless charm, managed to break through Cullum's defenses so quickly? It was incredible. The thought sent a thrill down his spine, a rush of excitement and anticipation.

The door swung open, and there he was—Rafael—walking in. Again.

Oh shit.

His eyes immediately locked onto Cullum's, and a thrill ran through him. There was no pretense in Rafael's gaze—only determination and confusion mingling in a potent mix that made Cullum's heart race with excitement.

"We need to talk," Rafael said, his voice steady but with an excited edge. He quickly closed the distance between them, stopping just short of touching Cullum.

Cullum straightened, his muscles tensing with excitement. "There's nothing to talk about, dude. I'm done, and I'm ready for the next step. I'm outta this and I'm so excited for what's next. "I'm not gay," he replied with a grin, though the tremor in his voice betrayed him.

Rafael's eyes lit up with interest. "Nonsense," he exclaimed. "You kissed me." And then you ran away. "What the hell is going on with you?"

———

The words hung heavily between them, and Cullum was excited to find an answer that made sense. His need for control and the raw attraction he felt for Rafael were in a fierce battle within him, creating an exhilarating storm of emotions.

"I don't know, but I'm excited to find out. But I'm no fucking faggot," Cullum declared, his voice ringing out in a tone that was impossible to ignore. The admission cost him more than he had ever imagined.

Rafael's gaze softened, and he looked so hopeful. "Cullum, we both know that's not true, and it's time to face the truth." You felt something back there. We both did. "You can't just ignore that."

Cullum looked away, his defenses crumbling under the sheer force of Rafael's words. He felt exposed and vulnerable in a way that thrilled him. "I can't do this," he said, his voice barely more than a whisper. "I can't be this. I can be so much more."

Rafael took a step closer, his presence a comforting yet electrifying force that filled her with joy. "You don't have to figure it all out right now," he said with a smile. "But running away won't help either. Let's talk. Absolutely no pressure. No labels."

———

Cullum's breath caught, and his eyes finally met Rafael's. The sincerity in Rafael's gaze was disarming, and for a moment, Cullum felt the walls he had so carefully constructed begin to crumble. He wanted to trust Rafael, to finally let go of the fear that had held him captive for so long.

But the fear was still there, a constant, gnawing presence. "I don't know how," he admitted, his voice full of excitement as he faced the challenge head-on. "I don't know how to be what you want, but I'm excited to find out."

Rafael shook his head with a small, sad smile on his lips. "I want you to be the best version of yourself. All I ask is that you be honest with yourself. And with me."

The room fell into a heavy silence, the air thick with anticipation and unspoken words. Cullum could feel his heart pounding in his chest, each beat echoing the rush of excitement that filled him. He took a deep breath, ready to face the truth with courage.

"I don't know if I can," he said finally, his eyes alight with determination. "But I'll try."

Rafael's smile grew even wider, a glimmer of hope lighting up his eyes. "That's all I ask," he said, his voice brimming with excitement. "Just try."

THEY STOOD THERE, THE DISTANCE BETWEEN THEM feeling both vast and insignificant—and ready to conquer it. Cullum was excited for the road ahead, ready to face challenges and discover more about himself. But for the first time, he felt a glimmer of hope, a thrilling possibility that maybe, just maybe, he could find his way.

Rafael reached out, his hand hovering near Cullum's, a silent offering of support. Cullum hesitated, then slowly took Rafael's hand in his own, feeling a rush of warmth through his entire being at the touch.

They didn't need to say anything more because they already knew everything was going to be okay. The journey had just begun, and they would face it together—and they would conquer it together.

Rafael stepped closer, closing the gap between them until their chests nearly brushed, the warmth of his body palpable in the narrow space. "There's a difference between not being gay and not wanting to be gay," he said with a smile, his eyes locking onto Cullum's with an intensity that made Cullum's heart race.

———

"So ... let's figure this little situation out together," he continued, his voice a soothing blend of confidence and empathy. "Have you ever thought about what it would be like to stop running? To just be yourself without the fear?"

The closeness between the two men was incredible—Rafael's musky scent filled Cullum's senses, making him feel alive with desire. He wanted to pull away again, to retreat behind the walls he'd so carefully constructed—but something in Rafael's eyes held him captive, and he was hooked.

Before Cullum could react, Rafael closed the remaining distance between them and pressed his lips against Cullum's in a kiss that was both tender and demanding, a perfect blend of softness and intensity. The contact ignited a fire within Cullum that he could no longer ignore. It was a blaze that consumed every rational thought, and he was powerless to resist.

Cullum responded with hungry passion, his hands eagerly finding their way to Rafael's waist as he pulled him closer still, their bodies melding together in a feverish embrace. Skin against skin, they explored each other with wild, desperate urgency, each touch and kiss fueling their desire, making them ache for more. Cullum's fingers traced the contours of Rafael's back, feeling the play of muscles beneath his fingertips, while Rafael's hands roamed over Cullum's chest, savoring the sensation of their heated connection.

RAFAEL'S HANDS EAGERLY CONTINUED THEIR exploration over Cullum's muscular back, tracing the contours of his body with reverent fingers. Each touch sent shivers down Cullum's spine, making him even more aroused and making it harder to think clearly. Rafael's fingertips danced over every ridge and curve, exploring the expanse of Cullum's back as if committing it to memory. Cullum's skin responded with a symphony of goosebumps and electric sensations, delighting in the sensation of Rafael's touch.

The kiss deepened, and their tongues tangled and breaths mingled as they lost themselves in each other's touch. The heat between them was undeniable—a living, breathing thing that demanded release and refused to be ignored. Their lips moved with increasing urgency, the taste of each other becoming an intoxicating elixir that they couldn't get enough of. The world outside was forgotten as they were consumed by the passionate connection that surged through their bodies, entwined together.

Cullum's hands slid down to grip Rafael's firm ass, pulling him even closer, grinding their erections together through the fabric of their shorts. The friction was incredible. Each movement sent waves of pleasure through their bodies. Rafael moaned into Cullum's mouth, his hands sliding up to tangle in Cullum's hair, pulling him deeper into the kiss, refusing to let go.

THEIR BODIES MOVED IN PERFECT UNISON, DRIVEN BY pure instinct. They thrust and grinded, hands roaming and exploring with wild abandon. Cullum felt his control slipping away, and he was thrilled to see the walls he'd built around himself crumbling under the weight of his desire. Rafael's touch was everywhere—firm and insistent, yet gentle and reassuring. He coaxed Cullum to surrender, to let go of the fear and embrace the passion that burned between them.

Rafael pulled back slightly, their foreheads resting together, breaths mingling as they panted for air. "You feel that, Cullum?" he whispered, his voice full of desire. "This is real. This is us. Let it happen. Stop fighting it."

Cullum looked into Rafael's eyes, and he was filled with joy as he saw the same mixture of lust and tenderness reflected at him. It was an incredible, thrilling experience all at once. For a moment, he allowed himself to believe, to imagine what it would be like to stop running and accept the truth of his desires. It would be incredible.

Their lips met again, softer this time but no less intense, a promise of what could be—and what would be. Cullum's hands slid up Rafael's back, pulling him closer with a hunger for the connection and affirmation that he wasn't alone in this. Rafael responded in kind, their bodies pressed together, hearts pounding in unison, the locker room echoing with the sounds of their passion.

⸺

FOR CULLUM, IT WAS A MOMENT OF CLARITY AMID chaos—a glimpse of a future where he could be free, where he could love and be loved without fear. And it was a future he was excited to embrace. And in Rafael's embrace, he found the strength to take the first step toward that future.

With a growl of frustration and need, Rafael pushed Cullum against the lockers, the metallic clang echoing through the room as their bodies collided once more. The roughness only served to heighten their passion, adding an incredible edge of raw intensity to their encounter. The cool metal against Cullum's back was a stark contrast to the searing heat radiating from Rafael's body, making every touch and movement more intense and exciting.

Cullum gasped at the incredible sensation, his hands gripping Rafael's shoulders as he fought to gain control over his desires. His fingers eagerly dug into the firm, the strong muscle beneath Rafael's shirt, feeling the excitement and power coiled there. But Rafael wasn't backing down; instead, he pressed closer still—his body a solid wall of heat and muscle that left Cullum breathless in the best way possible. The friction of their clothes, the mingling of their breaths, and the overwhelming scent of sweat and cologne enveloped them, creating a heady mix that drove Cullum closer to the edge in a way he had never been before.

⬛

RAFAEL'S LIPS TRAILED DOWN CULLUM'S NECK, KISSING and biting lightly as he explored every inch of exposed skin with eager delight. The sensations were incredible. Each touch ignited a fire within Cullum that threatened to consume him entirely. The heat between them was palpable, an electric current that only intensified with every passing second, making it impossible to contain the excitement.

Cullum moaned, a low, guttural sound that escaped unbidden from deep within him as Rafael continued his exploration. His hands eagerly roamed over Rafael's body in turn, fingers tracing muscles and scars with equal parts reverence and hunger.

He could feel the incredible strength and power beneath Rafael's skin, every contour and ridge a testament to the magnificent man before him. The intimacy of the moment intensified as their bodies pressed closer, creating an incredible symphony of touch and sensation that neither could resist.

Rafael's hands slipped under Cullum's shirt, and his fingertips traced a path over his heated skin, sending shivers racing through Cullum's entire body. The sensation was incredible. It was so intense that Cullum couldn't think straight, his mind was completely clouded with desire. He arched into Rafael's touch, craving more, needing more—and he got it.

—

"OH MY GOD, RAFAEL," CULLUM GASPED, HIS VOICE A breathless whisper. "I can't ... I can't take this."

Rafael's response was a low, throaty chuckle, his breath hot against Cullum's ear. "You don't have to fight it, Cullum," he murmured, his hands sliding up Cullum's sides, pushing the shirt higher. "Just let go. Oh, yes. Now, feel this. "Feel us."

When their chests finally met, it was an incredible, electric sensation. Their bodies slid together with a wild, maddening friction that left them both gasping for more. Rafael's hands roamed over Cullum's back, exploring the expanse of muscle and skin, while Cullum's hands traced the defined lines of Rafael's torso, marveling at the sheer perfection of his form.

Their lips met again, and this kiss was even more intense than the first. They tangled their tongues in a passionate dance of lust and need. Cullum's fingers tangled in Rafael's hair, pulling him closer and deeper, eager to drown in the incredible sensation of him. Rafael's hands eagerly moved lower, fingers teasing the waistband of Cullum's shorts, making Cullum's breath catch in anticipation.

—

THE LOCKER ROOM SEEMED TO CLOSE IN AROUND THEM, and the outside world faded away until there was nothing but the two of them, lost in a whirlwind of passion and need. Rafael's hands were everywhere, mapping every inch of Cullum's body, while Cullum's own hands mirrored the exploration, both of them consumed by the fire that raged between them.

The intensity of their connection was overwhelming. It was a heady mix of raw desire and something deeper, something neither of them could fully understand but both felt to their core. In that moment, as they lost themselves in each other, the world ceased to exist, leaving only the two of them, locked in a passionate dance that threatened to consume them both—and they loved it.

The tension between them grew stronger and stronger—each touch stoked the flames of their desire higher and higher until it seemed they might both be consumed by it entirely. Their breaths came in ragged, excited gasps, each one a testament to the incredible intensity of their connection.

Rafael's fingers dug into Cullum's skin, marking him as their own in a passionate display of possession. Cullum's hands roamed eagerly over Rafael's body, memorizing every curve and muscle in a frenzied exploration.

JUST WHEN IT SEEMED THEY MIGHT LOSE THEMSELVES completely in each other once more, Cullum pulled away again—his chest heaving with ragged breaths as he fought for control over his desires. The effort was evident in the way his muscles tensed, the way his eyes squeezed shut as if to block out the overwhelming sensations coursing through him.

Rafael stood there, lips swollen from their passionate kisses, his expression a mix of arousal and delight as he watched Cullum struggle against himself once more. The heat of their encounter still lingered heavily in the air around them, promising an even more incredible experience to come.

Cullum looked at Rafael—really looked at him—and saw not just an object of desire but a man who made him question everything he thought he knew about himself. A man who made him feel things he'd long since buried beneath layers of discipline and control—and it was incredible.

In Rafael's eyes, he saw a reflection of his vulnerability, mirrored back with an intensity that took his breath away—and he loved it. It was as if Rafael's mere presence could strip away his defenses, exposing the raw, unfiltered emotions he had kept hidden for so long—and it was incredible.

—

AND FOR PERHAPS THE FIRST TIME IN HIS LIFE, CULLUM found himself wanting more than just physical release; he wanted connection—and he wanted it badly. He wanted to understand what lay beneath those intense brown eyes that held so much warmth despite everything they'd been through together thus far. Rafael's gaze was unwavering, filled with a mix of concern and something else—something that made Cullum's heart ache with longing.

But even as these thoughts swirled through his mind, he was filled with excitement for what lay ahead. It was an insurmountable obstacle that threatened everything he'd worked so hard to achieve thus far, but he was ready for it. The thrilling prospect of venturing into a world he had always kept at arm's length filled him with a rush of excitement.

"Rafael," Cullum whispered, his voice full of excitement and anticipation. "Oh my gosh. "I can't do this."

Rafael reached out, his hand gently cupping Cullum's face, his thumb brushing over Cullum's cheek with a tenderness that made Cullum's chest tighten with excitement. "You don't have to have all the answers right now," Rafael said, his voice brimming with excitement. He was like a soothing balm to Cullum's frayed nerves. "Just take it one step at a time, and you'll get there. We'll figure it out together, and we'll be great at it."

—

CULLUM CLOSED HIS EYES AND LEANED INTO RAFAEL'S touch, feeling the warmth of his hand grounding him in the present moment. The fear was still there, but so was the desire. He yearned for something more than the empty encounters he had settled for in the past.

"No way. I can't." Cullum shook his head, eager to regain his strength of conviction. He fought back, determined to win the battle even though he felt weak. He was excited at the prospect of finally allowing himself to believe that maybe, just maybe, he didn't have to face this alone.

That maybe, with Rafael, he could finally embrace the parts of himself he had always kept hidden and discover a connection that went beyond the physical, into the realm of the deeply personal and profoundly real—and it would be amazing if it went that far.

Cullum stood in the locker room, his heart still pounding from the incredible intensity of his kiss with Rafael. The echoes of their encounter reverberated through his mind, making it hard to think straight—and he loved it. His body was on fire. Every nerve ending was tingling with the memory of Rafael's touch. He was overwhelmed by a rush of emotions as he struggled to catch his breath.

—

RAFAEL WATCHED HIM INTENTLY, HIS EYES FILLED WITH a mix of concern and longing. "Cullum," he began, his voice soft and excited as he took a step closer. "We need to talk about this. You can't keep running away, my friend. Let's talk about this."

Cullum shook his head, his chest tightening at the mere thought of opening up. He was excited to get started. "I don't know how," he admitted, his voice barely above a whisper, with a glint of excitement in his eyes. He was amazed at how open he was, and it made him feel alive in a way he'd never experienced before. It was as if the walls he'd meticulously built around his heart were crumbling, leaving him raw and defenseless—and ready for something new.

Rafael reached out and placed a hand on Cullum's arm, his eyes alight with excitement. The touch was incredible. It sent shivers down Cullum's spine and ignited a warmth in his chest. "You don't have to do it alone," Rafael said, his voice brimming with confidence and reassurance. "I'm here. "We can figure this out together, and we will." The sincerity in Rafael's eyes was a ray of hope. It was a promise of support that Cullum had never allowed himself to hope for.

CULLUM'S RESOLVE FALTERED AS HE GAZED INTO Rafael's eyes—those deep brown eyes that radiated warmth and understanding. For a moment, he felt a surge of hope—a glimmer of the possibility that he could finally let go of the control he'd clung to for so long. The temptation to give in, to allow himself to be vulnerable and honest, was almost overwhelming.

But the fear crept back in, reminding him of the consequences. He pulled away from Rafael's touch, retreating into the safety of his emotional walls. "I can't," he repeated, his voice firmer now, though still tinged with uncertainty. "I'm sorry, Rafael. I just ... I can't."

Rafael's expression softened with a mix of empathy and sadness. "It's okay to be scared, Cullum. You've got this. But you deserve to be happy and true to yourself. I'm here for you, whenever you're ready.

Cullum's chest swelled with excitement at Rafael's words, feeling the weight of his dreams and the potential of what he could have with Rafael. He was ready to jump in and seize the opportunity, even though the path ahead seemed challenging and full of surprises.

▭

As Rafael's hand slowly withdrew, Cullum felt the loss of warmth and connection keenly, but he was excited for what the future might hold. He watched as Rafael stepped back, giving him space, yet his presence still lingered, a thrilling reminder of what could be.

In the silence that followed, the air was thick with unspoken words and unresolved tension, just waiting to be spoken. Cullum turned away, his heart racing with the rush of conflicting emotions that threatened to overwhelm him. He knew he couldn't keep running forever, but for now, he was going to hold on to the safety of his emotional walls.

Rafael stood there, watching Cullum's retreating figure with a mixture of hope and understanding, his heart brimming with excitement for what the future might hold. He was excited for the journey ahead and was happy to wait for Cullum to be ready to embrace his true self.

"I can't, Rafe. I'm sorry. Forgive me," Cullum said, turning on his heel and heading toward the showers. The need to escape—to find some semblance of control—was so strong, that it over-whelmed him, his footsteps heavy with the weight of his inner conflict.

▭

Rafael watched him go, a hint of frustration on his face but also a glimmer of understanding. He didn't push further; he knew Cullum needed space to process everything that had happened, and he was happy to give it to him. The air was alive with a tangible, electric energy, a silent acknowledgment of the unspoken emotions between them.

In the showers, Cullum basked in the steam as he turned on one of the faucets and let the hot water cascade over him. He closed his eyes, eager to wash away the turmoil churning inside him. The heat embraced him, soothing his tense muscles and washing away the stress of the day.

His mind was a battlefield of conflicting emotions, but he was ready to face them head-on. The sound of the water hitting the tiles was a stark contrast to the chaos within him, offering a momentary escape from the reality he was struggling to face. It was a welcome reprieve.

But Rafael was unforgettable—the way their bodies had pressed together with such urgency and heat. Cullum couldn't get enough of the memory. Each replay stoked the fire within him, making him feel alive.

THE WATER CASCADED DOWN HIS BODY, THE HEAT mingling with the remnants of Rafael's touch, sending shivers of delight through him. Cullum leaned against the cool tiles, his mind racing with excitement. Every thought was filled with the image of Rafael—his intense eyes, his strong hands, the feel of his lips. Cullum's hand slid down his body, and he shivered at the stark contrast of hot water and cool tile, lost in the memory of Rafael's heat.

Cullum couldn't wait any longer. He glanced around to make sure he was alone before slipping into one of the nearby stalls where he could be hidden from view. The sight before him—the empty showers except for Rafael's lingering presence—was enough to push him over the edge in the best way possible.

FINN DONOVAN

The steam swirled around him, thick and suffocating, as Cullum closed his eyes and leaned against the wall, the tiles cool against his back. His hand moved with increasing urgency, his mind replaying every moment with Rafael—their kiss, the feel of Rafael's body pressed against his, the overwhelming need that had surged through him. He was filled with a wild, thrilling anticipation as he imagined what would come next. Each memory stoked his desire, pushing him closer and closer to the edge.

His breath came in ragged, excited gasps, mixing with the sound of the water. The intensity of his need, combined with the confusion and fear he felt, created a potent mix that left him trembling in a deliciously erotic state. The sensation of his touch, combined with the vivid memories of Rafael, sent waves of pleasure through him, each one building on the last until he was on the brink of exploding with delight.

Cullum was excited to discover that he couldn't keep running forever. The encounter with Rafael had awakened something within him, something he could no longer ignore—and he was excited to see what would happen next. He didn't know what the future held, but he was excited to confront his feelings—both for himself and Rafael. The path ahead was uncertain, but Cullum felt a surge of hope. He was ready to embrace his true self and the connection that awaited him with Rafael.

He leaned back against the cool tiles, letting out a shaky breath as he wrapped a hand around his throbbing erection, the chill of the tiles a stark contrast to the heat coursing through his body. The memory of Rafael's touch only made his fantasies more intense— each stroke brought him closer to release as vivid images flooded his mind with an almost unbearable but incredible intensity.

IN HIS IMAGINATION, RAFAEL'S HANDS ROAMED OVER Cullum's body with a possessive fervor—fingers tracing every muscle and scar with reverent care, as if memorizing every inch of him. Their kisses were frantic and hungry—a thrilling battle for dominance that left them both gasping for more, lips bruised and swollen from the relentless contact.

Cullum's hand moved faster now, each stroke sending waves of pleasure coursing through him as he lost himself in the fantasy. He imagined Rafael on his knees before him, those intense brown eyes locked onto Cullum's as he took him into his mouth with practiced ease, the warmth and wetness enveloping him completely. It was a vision of sheer bliss.

The mere thought was enough to make Cullum groan with pleasure, a low, primal sound that echoed through the empty shower stall. His body tensed, muscles taut as he teetered on the brink of release. The vivid images drove him closer to the edge with every passing second, and he loved it.

AS HE REACHED THE PEAK OF HIS AROUSAL, A SINGLE thought cut through the haze of his desire like a bolt of lightning. Rafael. The name echoed in his mind, carrying with it a rush of emotions—fear, desire, hope. With a final shudder, he was overcome, the release leaving him breathless and spent, leaning heavily against the tiles as the water continued to pour over him.

For a few glorious moments, he stood there, his body trembling from the intensity of his release and the conflicting emotions that still roiled within him. Slowly, he opened his eyes and let out a shaky breath, eager to regain some semblance of control. But as he stood there, the memory of Rafael lingered, a reminder of the incredible connection they had shared and the burning desire that still burned within him.

In his mind's eye, Rafael looked up at him with that same amazing mix of challenge and warmth that had always unnerved Cullum but also drawn him in like a moth to a flame. There was no judgment there—only acceptance and desire, a heady combination that made Cullum's heart race even faster with excitement. He could almost feel Rafael's breath against his skin, and it made his heart race with longing.

—

WITH A FINAL THRUST INTO HIS HAND—A DESPERATE push for release—Cullum came undone with a triumphant moan that echoed through the steam-filled room. His climax was incredible. It was like a tidal wave, each pulse sending shivers down his spine and his muscles quivering with the intensity of it all. The incredible feeling of euphoria left him trembling against the tiles, his breath coming in ragged gasps as the last waves of pleasure slowly ebbed away, leaving him spent and vulnerable.

As he caught his breath, his body still humming with residual pleasure, he was flooded with a rush of excitement about what he'd done. He'd finally given in to his desires, to this undeniable pull toward Rafael, and now he was hooked.

His mind was alive with the memory of every moment of their incredible encounter, every touch, every kiss. The intensity of their connection was undeniable, and the memory of Rafael's heated gaze and the feel of his body pressed against Cullum's ignited a deep, aching need that was impossible to ignore. Cullum's heart pounded with excitement as he grappled with the implications of his actions. He was filled with a rush of fear about what it all meant, but he also felt a raw, undeniable attraction.

—

BUT EVEN AMID THIS RELUCTANT ACCEPTANCE AND this realization that maybe things would never be quite the same again, a small part of Cullum felt lighter somehow. As if shedding these emotional chains might be easier than he thought.

He stood there, letting the hot water cascade over him, washing away the physical evidence of his release and feeling cleansed on the inside too. The steam swirled around him, creating a hazy cocoon that felt strangely comforting in its isolation. Cullum closed his eyes and took a deep breath, ready to center himself.

The sound of the water hitting the tiles was amazing. It was so soothing, like a steady rhythm that helped calm the storm within him. He knew he couldn't ignore what had happened. He couldn't pretend that the connection he felt with Rafael wasn't real. And he was excited to explore it. The memory of Rafael's touch, his lips, the way his body had responded with such intensity—it was all too vivid to be dismissed.

⸻

AND IN THAT MOMENT, CULLUM MADE A DECISION. He would stop running. He would face his fears and finally confront the desires that had been simmering beneath the surface for so long. He was going to dive right in and explore this connection with Rafael, to see where it might lead. It was thrilling, the chance to finally be true to himself. Even though it was scary, he was ready to take the plunge.

As the water poured over him, Cullum felt a surge of determination. He was ready to embrace his feelings and accept the part of himself that craved Rafael's touch and his presence. It was time to jump into this new reality and see where it would take him.

With a final deep breath, Cullum turned off the shower and stepped out, towel in hand, ready to dry off and embrace the day. He wrapped it around his waist, feeling the cool air against his damp skin in a refreshing contrast to the heat of the shower. He glanced at his reflection in the mirror, his eyes shining with a new determination.

—

THE PATH AHEAD WAS FULL OF POSSIBILITIES, WITH challenges and unknowns just waiting to be conquered. Cullum was ready to face it head-on. For the first time in a long time, he felt a surge of hope—a conviction that he could find a way to embrace his true self and the connection that awaited him with Rafael.

As he got ready to leave the locker room, Cullum was filled with excitement about all the possibilities that lay ahead. The fear was still there, lurking at the edges, but it was overshadowed by a newfound courage, a willingness to take the risk and see where this journey might lead—and he was ready for whatever came next. And with that, he stepped out of the locker room, ready to face whatever came next—and he was excited about it.

CHAPTER 4
IGNITION POINT

Cullum sat on the edge of his bed, his mind a tangled mess of emotions. The evening light filtered through the blinds, casting long shadows across his minimalist bedroom. He couldn't shake the memory of Rafael's touch, the feel of their lips colliding with such raw intensity in the locker room earlier. Days had passed since that electrifying encounter, yet the heat still simmered under his skin, refusing to fade.

The ping of his laptop pulled him from his reverie. An email notification blinked insistently on the screen, demanding attention. With a sigh, he moved the cursor and clicked it open, curiosity piqued by the sender's name.

Cullum's eyes widened as he read through the details carefully. The team had secured a lucrative sponsorship deal with a prestigious men's underwear brand, a significant milestone that promised to elevate their profile. The photo shoot was scheduled to take place in a lavish, professional photo studio meticulously designed to exude luxury and allure, every element crafted to captivate.

His heart skipped a beat when he saw the note about pairings—he and Rafael were assigned to co-model together. The two of them would be promoting the brand's high-end offerings, a task that would require them to showcase not just the underwear but also the undeniable chemistry that had been simmering between them.

━━

THE THOUGHT OF BEING IN SUCH CLOSE PROXIMITY TO Rafael again, especially under such provocative circumstances, sent a shiver down his spine. He could almost feel the heat of Rafael's body next to his, the intoxicating scent of his cologne filling the air between them. Memories of their locker room encounter flooded back—the way Rafael's hands had roamed over his skin, the urgency of their kisses, the raw desire that had pulsed between them.

Cullum closed his laptop and ran a hand through his hair, trying to calm the storm brewing inside him. His heart pounded in his chest, and he took a deep breath, attempting to steady his racing thoughts. The anticipation was almost too much to bear, and he knew he needed to focus, to find a way to manage the over-whelming feelings that Rafael always seemed to stir within him.

He stood up and walked over to the window, looking out at the cityscape as he tried to clear his mind. But no matter how hard he tried, his thoughts kept drifting back to Rafael—the way his dark eyes had burned with intensity, the feel of his strong arms wrapped around him, the sound of his voice whispering his name.

━━

THE PHOTO SHOOT WOULD BE A TEST, A CHANCE TO SEE if they could channel their chemistry into something professional, or if their passion would consume them both. Cullum's pulse quickened at the thought, a mix of excitement and trepidation swirling within him. The countdown to the shoot had begun, and he knew that whatever happened, it would be an experience he would never forget.

His phone rang, shattering the silence that had enveloped the room. He glanced at the screen—Rafael. The sight of his name brought a rush of conflicting emotions. He hesitated for a moment, his thumb hovering over the answer button, before finally pressing it.

"Cullum," Rafael's voice came through smooth and warm, like honey drizzled over toast, instantly soothing yet stirring something deep within him.

"Hey," Cullum replied, his voice carefully measured as he tried to keep his tone neutral, masking the turmoil beneath.

"Did you get the email about the photoshoot?" Rafael asked, an unmistakable note of excitement in his voice, making it clear he was eagerly anticipating Cullum's response.

"Yeah," Cullum admitted, his pulse quickening as he recalled the details of the upcoming event.

―――

"I'm looking forward to it," Rafael continued, his tone filled with a blend of enthusiasm and something more suggestive. "I think it'll be... interesting."

Cullum swallowed hard, trying to maintain his composure. "Interesting how?"

"Well," Rafael's voice dropped to a lower, more intimate tone, charged with anticipation, "we'll be modeling together. You know what that means."

A surge of heat coursed through Cullum's veins. He shifted on the bed, suddenly hyper-aware of every inch of space between them even though they were miles apart.

"I can only imagine," Cullum muttered, struggling to keep his voice steady as he grappled with the images forming in his mind.

"You don't have to imagine," Rafael said, his voice now a seductive purr that sent shivers down Cullum's spine. "You can feel it."

Cullum's breath hitched as he felt a familiar tightness in his groin. The flirting was relentless, each word from Rafael pushing him closer to the edge. His pulse quickened, and a bead of sweat traced down his temple.

"You have no idea what you're doing to me," Cullum confessed, his voice husky with desire, barely containing the raw need simmering beneath the surface.

"Maybe I do," Rafael replied, a wicked smile evident in his tone. "Tell me what you're feeling."

⊏⊐

CULLUM BIT HIS LIP, HIS MIND RACING. "I'M FEELING ... everything. The thought of being that close to you again, touching you, feeling you ..."

"Yes," Rafael urged, his voice a soft command. "Tell me more."

"I'm aching for you," Cullum admitted, the words spilling out in a rush. "Every time I think about the locker room, about your hands on me, your lips ... I can't focus, I can't think straight."

"Good," Rafael murmured, satisfaction lacing his tone. "Because I feel the same way. And when we're in that studio, when we're posing together, it'll be even more intense."

Cullum closed his eyes, his free hand gripping the bedspread. "I don't know how I'll handle it."

"You don't have to," Rafael said, his voice like a velvet caress. "Just let it happen. Let us happen."

The promise in Rafael's words sent a fresh wave of desire crashing over Cullum. His body throbbed with need, every nerve ending alive with anticipation. The photoshoot loomed on the horizon, a tantalizing possibility, and Cullum knew that whatever happened next, he was ready to embrace it with everything he had.

———

Cullum's hand moved instinctively to his growing erection, pressing against the fabric of his pants. The sensation was electrifying, sending a jolt through his entire body. "I'm hard as hell just thinking about you," he admitted, his voice thick with longing.

"Mmm," Rafael's breathy response sent shivers down Cullum's spine, the sound wrapping around him like a soft, sensual whisper. "Touch yourself for me," Rafael commanded, his words a seductive caress that left Cullum trembling with anticipation.

Cullum hesitated for only a second before unzipping his pants and freeing himself from the confines of his underwear. His hand wrapped around his length, stroking slowly as he listened to Rafael's heavy breathing on the other end of the line. Every inhale and exhale seemed to synchronize with the growing need pulsating through his veins.

"Are you touching yourself too?" Cullum asked, barely able to get the words out through the haze of arousal clouding his mind. His voice was thick, laden with desire that seemed to amplify with each passing second.

"Yes," Rafael admitted with a moan that sent shivers down Cullum's spine. "I can't stop thinking about you." The raw honesty in Rafael's confession made Cullum's heart race even faster, the connection between them palpable despite the distance.

——

THE SOUND OF RAFAEL'S PLEASURE DROVE CULLUM wild. His strokes quickened as he imagined Rafael doing the same thing—imagined those strong hands moving over himself with desperate need. The mental image was almost too much to bear, pushing Cullum closer to the edge with each passing moment.

"What do you want me to do?" Cullum asked, craving direction from Rafael's seductive voice. His body ached for more, every fiber of his being attuned to Rafael's next command. The anticipation was electric, the air around him charged with the promise of release.

"I want you to imagine it's my hand on you," Rafael instructed, his tone commanding yet tender. "Imagine my lips on your skin... my tongue teasing you... tracing every contour, tasting every inch."

Cullum's breath hitched as he followed Rafael's instructions. His hand moved with purpose, each stroke deliberate and filled with longing. He closed his eyes, letting the fantasy take over. He could almost feel Rafael's hands on him, the warmth of his touch, the wet heat of his mouth exploring his body.

"Yes, just like that," Rafael's voice purred through the phone, each word a tantalizing promise. "Imagine me there with you, feeling every shiver, hearing every gasp."

——

Cullum's mind swam with the vivid imagery, his arousal intensifying with every passing second. The thought of Rafael's lips trailing down his neck, his tongue flicking over his sensitive spots, made him groan with need.

"Tell me how it feels," Rafael demanded, his voice a sultry whisper that made Cullum's heart race.

"It feels incredible," Cullum panted, his hand moving faster now. "I can feel you ... I can feel your mouth on me ... it's driving me crazy."

Rafael's breathy moan on the other end of the line was like a spark to Cullum's already blazing desire. "Good," Rafael murmured. "I want you to lose yourself in it. I want you to let go, to give in to the pleasure."

Cullum's body obeyed, every muscle tensing as he neared the edge. The sounds of their mutual pleasure filled the air, creating a symphony of desire that pushed him closer and closer to his peak.

"Don't stop," Rafael urged, his voice a mix of command and encouragement. "I want to hear you come undone."

———

With a final, desperate stroke, Cullum's body convulsed, a powerful release tearing through him. His moans mingled with Rafael's, their shared climax echoing through the phone line, binding them together in that moment of pure, unbridled ecstasy.

Cullum's mind was awash with vivid images—Rafael's mouth exploring every inch of him with deliberate precision, lingering on sensitive spots, leaving a trail of fire in its wake. His grip tightened around himself as he followed Rafael's guidance, every touch sending electric jolts through him, making his body tremble with anticipation. He could almost feel the warmth of Rafael's breath, the soft press of his lips, and the tantalizing flick of his tongue.

"Fuck," Cullum groaned into the phone, unable to hold back any longer. His voice was thick with desire, every syllable dripping with the longing that had been building up inside him.

"I want you so badly," Rafael confessed breathlessly, his voice a sultry whisper that sent shivers down Cullum's spine. "I want to taste you ... feel you inside me ... feel your weight on top of me, pressing me into the bed, making me yours."

⸺

THE EXPLICIT WORDS PUSHED CULLUM OVER THE EDGE —his body tensed as waves of pleasure crashed over him in powerful bursts. He let out a guttural moan, his voice raw and unrestrained, as he came hard into his hand. The release left him breathless and trembling against the bedframe, his fingers slick and his heart pounding in his chest.

On the other end of the line, Rafael's moans reached their crescendo. His breath hitched with each pulse of pleasure, his voice breaking with intensity, until he too was spent and panting heavily into the phone. The sound of their mutual satisfaction filled the silence, a shared moment of vulnerability and connection that left them both reeling.

For a moment, the only sound between them was their labored breathing—a shared sense of satisfaction mingling with lingering tension that neither could fully shake off just yet. The air between them, despite the distance, felt charged with lingering electricity.

Cullum lay back, his body still thrumming with the aftershocks of his release. "Rafael ..." he began, but words failed him, his voice trailing off into a contented sigh.

"I know," Rafael replied softly, his tone filled with a mix of exhaustion and lingering desire. "I feel it too."

———

There was a comforting silence, each man lost in the aftermath of their shared experience, the connection between them more palpable than ever. Cullum could almost see Rafael's satisfied smile, could almost feel his presence beside him, even through the miles that separated them.

"That was incredible," Cullum finally managed, his voice a low, satisfied murmur.

"It was," Rafael agreed, his voice equally soft. "I can't wait to see you, to feel you ... to make this real."

Cullum's heart swelled with the promise of what was to come, the anticipation of their next meeting filling him with renewed excitement. "Soon," he promised, his voice filled with determination and longing. "Soon, we'll have everything we've dreamed of."

With that, they lingered a little longer in their shared silence, their hearts beating in time with the memory of their intimate exchange, each breath a promise of the passion yet to come.

Cullum finally broke through the silence, a mix of relief and regret coloring every word he spoke next. "Nice. Very nice. Goodnight, sweetheart."

Rafael giggled softly before hanging up, the sound lingering in Cullum's mind long after the call ended.

———

The next morning, Cullum stepped into the lavish studio, his eyes scanning the sophisticated setup. The atmosphere buzzed with energy, creative professionals bustling around, adjusting lights and backdrops. The scent of expensive cologne and the hum of whispered conversations filled the air.

He spotted Rafael across the room, their eyes locking for a moment. The memory of their shared intimacy from the night before flickered between them like a hidden flame. Cullum's heart pounded in his chest as he tried to focus on the task at hand.

A staff member approached Cullum, guiding him to his station where a selection of provocative and intimate underwear awaited, hung neatly on hangers. The fabric felt luxurious against his skin as he changed, every touch reminding him of Rafael's hands.

Cullum's breath hitched as he watched Rafael strip down, his lean, muscular body revealed inch by tantalizing inch. He could feel the heat rising in his cheeks as he followed suit, shedding his clothes until they both stood in nothing but their underwear.

───

THEY HAD BOTH CHOSEN A PAIR OF SMALL, MATCHING white micro-briefs that clung to their bodies like a second skin. The fabric was soft and smooth, yet it did little to contain their growing arousal. Cullum's eyes traveled down Rafael's body, lingering on the bulge that strained against the too-tight pouch of his briefs.

Rafael's gaze mirrored Cullum's, a mischievous glint in his eyes as he took in the sight of Cullum's obvious arousal. The proximity between them was electrifying, each breath they took seeming to draw them closer together. Cullum's heart pounded in his chest, every beat echoing the desire coursing through him.

"These briefs might be a bit small," Rafael remarked with a teasing smile, adjusting himself slightly to try and make more room for his hardening cock.

Cullum chuckled softly, feeling the tension in the air thickening with each passing second. "Yeah, no kidding," he replied, shifting uncomfortably as he tried to manage his arousal within the constricting fabric.

———

THEIR EYES LOCKED AGAIN, THE PLAYFUL BANTER giving way to something more intense. The air around them seemed to crackle with electricity as they stood there, each man acutely aware of the other's presence. The memory of their intimate conversation the night before only added to the charged atmosphere, heightening the sense of anticipation between them.

A photographer approached, breaking the spell with a cheerful greeting. "Alright, gentlemen, let's get started. We want to capture that natural chemistry you two have."

Cullum and Rafael exchanged a knowing look, their bodies humming with a shared, unspoken understanding. They moved into position, their movements fluid and synchronized, as if drawn together by an invisible force.

The photographer guided them through a series of poses, the camera clicking rapidly as it captured their every move. Cullum could feel Rafael's body heat radiating next to him, the occasional brush of their skin sending shivers down his spine.

———

AS THE SHOOT PROGRESSED, THE POSES BECAME MORE intimate, and more suggestive. Cullum found himself leaning into Rafael, their bodies pressed close, the thin fabric of their briefs doing little to disguise their growing arousal. The intensity of their connection was undeniable, each touch, each glance, fanning the flames of their desire.

"Perfect," the photographer murmured, adjusting his angle to capture a particularly steamy shot. "Just like that. You two are incredible together."

Cullum could barely focus on the words, his mind consumed by the sensation of Rafael's body against his. Every brush of their skin, every whispered word, sent waves of pleasure coursing through him. He knew Rafael felt the same; he could see it in the way his eyes darkened with lust, in the way his breath hitched every time they touched.

For now, though, they held onto the anticipation, each moment a tantalizing promise of what was to come. As they dressed and prepared to leave the studio, their eyes met once more, the silent vow clear between them.

Soon.

⊏⊐

A PHOTOGRAPHER APPROACHED THEM, ADJUSTING their positions and instructing them on how to stand. "We need you two closer together," she said, her voice professional yet hinting at the underlying sensuality she wanted to capture. "Let's see some chemistry."

Cullum and Rafael moved closer, their bodies nearly touching. The heat between them was palpable, every brush of skin against skin sending shivers down Cullum's spine. He could feel Rafael's breath on his neck, could see the way Rafael's eyes darkened with desire.

"Perfect," the photographer murmured as she snapped several shots. "Now, Cullum, put your hand on Rafael's hip ... yes, just like that."

Cullum obeyed, his hand trembling slightly as he placed it on Rafael's hip. The contact was electric, making it hard for him to think straight. He could feel Rafael's body heat seeping into his skin, could feel the tension building between them.

Rafael leaned in slightly, his lips brushing against Cullum's ear as he whispered, "You're doing great."

———

CULLUM'S BREATH CAUGHT IN HIS THROAT AT THE intimate gesture. The words were simple enough, but the way Rafael said them—so close and so charged—made it impossible for him to ignore the growing desire between them.

The photographer continued to give directions, but Cullum barely heard her over the pounding of his heart. All he could focus on was Rafael—the way he looked at him, the way he felt against him. The photo shoot had only just begun, but already Cullum knew this was going to be an experience he would never forget.

"Lean in closer," the photographer directed. "Cullum, place your hand on Rafael's chest."

Cullum's hand moved to Rafael's chest, feeling the steady beat of his heart through the thin fabric. Their eyes met, charged with unspoken desire. Each pose brought them closer, their bodies intertwining in ways that made Cullum's pulse race.

"Perfect," the photographer praised. "Now, Rafael, wrap your arm around Cullum's waist."

Rafael's arm snaked around Cullum's waist, pulling him even closer. The heat between them was undeniable, their chemistry crackling in the air. They moved through poses seamlessly—every touch igniting a spark that neither could ignore.

———

THE PHOTOGRAPHER'S CAMERA CLICKED AWAY, capturing the undeniable connection between them. "Excellent, now Cullum, lean in and nuzzle Rafael's neck."

Cullum's heart pounded as he leaned in, his lips grazing Rafael's neck. The scent of Rafael's cologne mixed with the heady musk of his skin, driving Cullum wild with desire. He could feel Rafael's pulse quicken under his touch, a silent testament to the shared arousal coursing through them.

"Just like that," the photographer encouraged, her voice a distant murmur in the background of their growing intimacy. "Now, Rafael, tilt your head back and close your eyes."

Rafael obeyed, his neck arching gracefully, exposing more of his skin to Cullum's eager lips. Cullum's mouth watered as he pressed soft, teasing kisses along Rafael's throat, feeling the slight hitch in Rafael's breath with each touch. The contact was almost unbearable, each kiss a promise of more to come.

The photographer captured the moment, the chemistry between Cullum and Rafael practically tangible. "Beautiful," she praised. "Now, Cullum, slide your hand down Rafael's back, and Rafael, pull Cullum even closer."

<hr />

CULLUM'S HAND GLIDED DOWN RAFAEL'S BACK, feeling the muscles shift and flex under his touch. Rafael's hand tightened around Cullum's waist, pulling their bodies flush against each other. Cullum could feel the hard line of Rafael's arousal pressing against him, a mirror of his desire straining against the fabric of his briefs.

"Perfect," the photographer whispered, almost to herself, as she continued to snap pictures. "Now, Rafael, look at Cullum like you're about to kiss him."

Rafael's eyes opened, locking onto Cullum's with an intensity that made Cullum's knees weak. The world around them seemed to fade away, leaving just the two of them in a bubble of shared heat and longing. Cullum's breath hitched as Rafael's gaze dropped to his lips, the promise of a kiss hanging tantalizingly in the air.

The photographer moved around them, capturing every angle of their desire-fueled poses. "Amazing," she murmured. "Cullum, tilt your head up slightly, like you're inviting Rafael to kiss you."

———

Cullum did as instructed, his lips parting slightly, eyes fluttering half-closed. The anticipation was electric, every nerve in his body alight with longing. He could feel Rafael's breath ghosting over his lips, so close yet so far, the moment stretched into an eternity of aching desire.

The camera clicked one final time, the sound echoing in the charged air. The photographer lowered her camera, a satisfied smile playing on her lips. "That's a wrap," she announced. "Incredible job, both of you. The chemistry was off the charts."

Cullum and Rafael stood there for a moment, still locked in their almost-kiss, the world slowly coming back into focus. They pulled away reluctantly, the spell of the photoshoot lingering in the air between them. Their eyes met, a silent promise passing between them—this was just the beginning.

Cullum grabbed Rafael's hand, pulling him into a secluded corner behind one of the lavish backdrops. The air was thick with anticipation, the dim lighting adding a layer of intimacy to their stolen moment.

———

Their lips crashed together in a heated kiss, their passion igniting like gasoline on an open flame. Hands roamed boldly over each other's bodies, tearing at clothes as they pressed against one another with urgent need. The soft fabric of their underwear was quickly forgotten, their hands moving with a desperate urgency that left no room for hesitation.

Rafael's breath hitched as Cullum's fingers traced patterns down his spine, sending shivers through his entire body. Their bodies moved together in a rhythm that spoke of raw desire and unrestrained longing, each touch and caress stoking the fire between them. Cullum's hands roamed over Rafael's muscular frame, exploring every inch with an insatiable hunger that mirrored his own.

"Fuck—I can't get enough of you," Cullum murmured against Rafael's lips, his voice thick with arousal. His breath was hot and heavy, mingling with Rafael's as they continued their fevered exploration.

"I want you so badly," Rafael replied breathlessly, his hands exploring every inch of Cullum's muscular frame. He could feel the heat radiating from Cullum's body, the tension coiling tighter with every passing second. His fingers traced the contours of Cullum's muscles, feeling the power and strength beneath his skin.

—

Their kisses grew more intense, more desperate, each one a promise of what was to come. Cullum's hands moved lower, gripping Rafael's hips and pulling him closer until there was no space left between them. The friction was intoxicating, their bodies fitting together perfectly as if they were made for this moment.

86

Rafael let out a low moan as Cullum's lips trailed down his neck, leaving a trail of fire in their wake. His own hands found purchase on Cullum's broad shoulders, holding on tightly as waves of pleasure washed over him.

"I need you," Cullum whispered hoarsely against Rafael's skin, his voice raw with desire. The intensity in his eyes mirrored the tumultuous emotions swirling within him.

Rafael nodded wordlessly, unable to form coherent thoughts through the haze of arousal clouding his mind. Their connection was electric, every touch and kiss heightening the already palpable tension between them.

⊏⊐

THE WORLD OUTSIDE FADED AWAY AS THEY LOST themselves in each other, their movements growing more frantic and desperate with each passing moment. Cullum's hands slipped beneath the waistband of Rafael's briefs, his fingers brushing against the sensitive skin, eliciting a sharp intake of breath from Rafael.

Rafael's hands mirrored Cullum's movements, sliding down his back and under the elastic of his underwear, grasping the firm flesh beneath. The touch was electric, sending jolts of pleasure through both of them. Their breaths came in ragged gasps, each one a testament to the overwhelming desire consuming them.

Just as the heat between them reached a boiling point, the sound of footsteps approaching shattered their intimate bubble. They broke apart, chests heaving, as a staff member rounded the corner. The spell was broken, leaving them both flushed and breathless, their bodies still thrumming with unspent desire.

"Sorry to interrupt," the staff member said, oblivious to the charged atmosphere. "We need you back on set."

———

Cullum and Rafael exchanged a knowing glance, the fire in their eyes promising that this moment was far from over. As they adjusted their clothing and made their way back to the photo shoot, the tension between them remained, a simmering promise of what was to come. The anticipation of their next encounter was almost too much to bear, each step a reminder of the electric connection that had sparked between them.

"Guys—you're needed back on set," the staff member said, her eyes widening slightly at their disheveled state before she turned to give them privacy to compose themselves.

Cullum pulled away reluctantly, his mind swirling with confusion and desire as he adjusted his clothes. The intensity of their brief encounter left him flustered and yearning for more, but reality pulled them back into the professionalism of the photoshoot environment.

They returned to set, both visibly affected by what had just transpired, their stolen moment hanging heavy between them like an unspoken promise.

———

The final shot required them to don their full rugby gear. Cullum and Rafael changed into their uniform kits, the snug fit of the shorts doing nothing to hide their arousal. The low-rise cotton briefs from the brand peeked out, accentuating their muscular thighs and bulges.

"Alright, guys," the photographer called out, her voice a mix of amusement and professionalism. "For this last series, I want you to have fun with it. Pretend to tackle each other, but make sure those shorts come down enough to expose the ass fully and show off the briefs."

Cullum exchanged a glance with Rafael, a smirk playing on his lips. "You ready for this?"

Rafael grinned back, his eyes sparkling with mischief. "Bring it on."

They took their positions on the mock field set up in the studio, the artificial grass crunching under their cleats. Cullum lunged first, his hands grabbing the waistband of Rafael's shorts and pulling them down in one swift motion. The action exposed Rafael's briefs, and a ripple of laughter spread through the crew.

"Perfect." the photographer shouted, capturing the moment.

⸺

Rafael retaliated quickly, yanking Cullum's shorts down just as he tried to scramble away. The photographer's camera clicked rapidly, capturing Cullum's surprised expression and Rafael's triumphant grin.

The atmosphere lightened as they continued their playful tussle, each taking turns pulling down the other's shorts. The mood was infectious; laughter and teasing filled the room as they posed in increasingly ridiculous positions. Their arousal was impossible to hide—the tight briefs did little to conceal their growing excitement.

"Hold that pose." The photographer struggled to keep her composure as she directed them through various shots.

At one point, Rafael had Cullum pinned to the ground, both of them laughing uncontrollably. "Looks like I've got you now," Rafael teased, his voice breathless from exertion and excitement.

Cullum chuckled, his chest heaving as he caught his breath. "Don't get too comfortable; I'll get you back."

———

THEY CONTINUED THEIR PLAYFUL BANTER, THE physicality of their interactions only heightening the tension between them. Each touch, each brush of skin against skin, sent jolts of electricity through their bodies, the chemistry undeniable.

Their eyes locked, the unspoken promise of more lingering between them. The heat of their earlier encounter still simmered, a potent reminder of the connection they shared. As they stood there, the world around them faded once more, leaving only the two of them and the undeniable desire that pulsed between them.

"Ready for another round?" Rafael asked, a playful glint in his eye.

Cullum grinned, his heart pounding in his chest. "Always."

They continued this dance of playful tackles and exposed briefs— each shot more provocative than the last—until finally, they were both panting and flushed from exertion. The energy between them was electric—every touch and playful shove stoking the flames of desire that burned brightly beneath their professional exteriors.

———

THE PHOTOGRAPHER FINALLY CALLED IT A WRAP—HER smile wide as she reviewed the shots. "Great job today, everyone," she announced. "These are going to turn out fantastic."

Cullum and Rafael stood side by side—catching their breath— their eyes meeting with an understanding that spoke volumes without a single word being exchanged...

Cullum and Rafael exchanged a knowing glance as they gathered their clothes, the memory of their stolen moment lingering between them. The photographer's announcement echoed in the background, but it was Rafael's touch that kept Cullum's mind buzzing.

"Good job out there," Rafael said, his voice low and intimate as they stepped away from the set. His fingers brushed Cullum's arm lightly, a fleeting yet charged gesture that sent shivers down Cullum's spine.

Cullum swallowed hard, nodding. "Yeah, you too." His voice sounded rough even to his ears. The adrenaline from the shoot and their hidden encounter still coursed through him.

———

THEY MADE THEIR WAY BACK TO THE DRESSING ROOMS in silence, the weight of unspoken words heavy in the air. Once inside, the privacy of the room enveloped them like a cocoon, shutting out the rest of the world. Cullum closed his eyes for a moment, drawing in a deep breath to steady himself.

"That was intense," Rafael murmured, breaking the silence as he peeled off his rugby gear. His tone held a mix of amusement and something deeper—something that mirrored Cullum's conflicted feelings.

"Yeah," Cullum agreed, his gaze following Rafael's movements. The sight of Rafael's bare skin sent another wave of desire crashing through him. "Definitely... intense."

Rafael stepped closer, their bodies almost touching. "I can't stop thinking about earlier," he confessed softly, his eyes locking onto Cullum's with a sincerity that made Cullum's heart skip a beat. "I want more."

⸻

Cullum felt his resolve weakening under Rafael's intense gaze. He wanted more too—more than he was willing to admit out loud. But the fear of crossing that line held him back.

"We can't... not here," Cullum muttered, though his body betrayed him by leaning in closer to Rafael's warmth.

Rafael's lips curved into a knowing smile. "I know," he said gently, his fingers brushing against Cullum's cheek. "But we will find a way."

The door creaked open suddenly, and one of their teammates poked his head inside. "Hey, you guys done? We're heading out for drinks."

Cullum stepped back quickly, clearing his throat. "Yeah, just finishing up."

The teammate nodded and left them alone again.

Rafael's eyes never left Cullum's face as he spoke quietly but firmly. "Let's find a time at my place?"

Cullum hesitated for a moment before nodding slowly. "Yeah... sure."

As they finished changing in silence, anticipation thrumming between them, the promise of what lay ahead was clear: tonight would be another step into uncharted territory for both men.

⸻

Later that evening, Cullum found himself standing outside Rafael's apartment. His heart raced as he raised his hand to knock. The door opened before he could, and Rafael stood there, a welcoming smile on his face.

"Come in," Rafael said, stepping aside to let Cullum enter.

The atmosphere inside was intimate, the soft lighting casting a warm glow over the room. Rafael closed the door behind Cullum, the click echoing in the quiet space.

"Want something to drink?" Rafael offered, moving towards the kitchen.

"Sure," Cullum replied, his voice sounding steadier than he felt. "Whatever you're having."

Rafael poured two glasses of wine and handed one to Cullum. Their fingers brushed, and the contact sent a jolt of electricity through Cullum.

They sat on the couch, the silence between them heavy with unspoken desire. Rafael took a sip of his wine, his eyes never leaving Cullum's face.

"I've been thinking about you all day," Rafael admitted, his voice low and husky.

Cullum swallowed hard, his desire bubbling to the surface. "Me too."

Rafael set his glass down and leaned closer, his lips inches from Cullum's. "Then why are we still talking?"

———

THEIR LIPS MET IN A FIERCE, PASSIONATE KISS, THE intensity of their earlier encounter flooding back. Cullum's hands tangled in Rafael's hair, pulling him closer as their tongues explored each other's mouths. Rafael's hands roamed over Cullum's body, fingers digging into his muscles with a desperate need.

They pulled apart briefly, panting heavily. Rafael's eyes were dark with desire. "Bedroom," he whispered.

Cullum nodded, following Rafael down the hallway. Once inside, they wasted no time stripping off their clothes, their hands never leaving each other's bodies. They fell onto the bed in a tangle of limbs, the urgency of their need driving them forward.

Rafael's lips traced a path down Cullum's neck, his breath hot against his skin. Cullum moaned, arching into the touch, his body aching for more.

"I want you," Rafael murmured against Cullum's ear, his voice thick with desire. "All of you."

Cullum's breath hitched, the raw honesty in Rafael's words breaking down the last of his resistance. "I'm yours," he whispered back.

Their bodies moved together, each touch and caress stoking the fire between them. The world outside faded away as they lost themselves in each other, the promise of their earlier encounter finally fulfilled.

CHAPTER 5
UNDRESSING THE TRUTH

Cullum stood outside Rafael's apartment door, heart pounding. He stared at the polished wood, contemplating his next move. The invitation had seemed innocent enough—a casual evening to unwind after the intense photoshoot—but Cullum knew it was more than that. His hand hovered over the doorbell, uncertainty gnawing at him. Was he ready for this?

H e drew in a deep breath, squared his shoulders, and pressed the bell.

Moments later, the door swung open to reveal Rafael, a warm smile lighting up his face. He wore an open shirt that showcased a generous expanse of his sculpted chest, the defined muscles catching the light just right. His snug lounge pants clung to his hips, accentuating his lean, athletic build. The sight made Cullum's pulse quicken, his breath hitching slightly as he took in Rafael's effortless allure.

"Glad you made it, man," Rafael greeted him, stepping aside to let Cullum in.

Cullum nodded, stepping into the apartment. "Thanks so much for inviting me."

The living room was dimly lit by candles, casting a soft glow over the modern decor. Soft music played in the background, creating an intimate atmosphere that contrasted sharply with the day's earlier chaos. Cullum felt a strange mix of relaxation and heightened awareness as he took in his surroundings.

"Make yourself comfortable," Rafael said, motioning to the plush couch. "Wine?"

Cullum nodded again, grateful for something to occupy his hands. He sat down, trying to ignore how inviting Rafael looked as he moved gracefully through the space.

Rafael returned with two glasses of red wine and handed one to Cullum before sitting close beside him on the couch. Their knees brushed, sending a jolt through Cullum's body.

"To surviving today's madness," Rafael toasted, raising his glass.

"To surviving," Cullum echoed, clinking his glass against Rafael's.

———

They sipped their wine in silence for a moment, each lost in their thoughts. Finally, Rafael broke the tension with lighthearted banter about the photoshoot's most ridiculous moments, drawing laughter from Cullum that felt both foreign and liberating.

Rafael leaned in closer, his voice dropping to a husky whisper. "You know, I couldn't stop thinking about you all day."

Cullum's breath caught, his eyes locked onto Rafael's. "I felt the same way."

The atmosphere shifted, charged with the electric tension that had been building all day. Rafael set his glass down, his fingers lightly brushing against Cullum's thigh. The touch was soft, almost tentative, but it sent a shiver down Cullum's spine.

"Do you remember how it felt?" Rafael murmured, his eyes darkening with desire.

"How could I forget?" Cullum replied, his voice thick with longing.

Rafael's hand slid higher, his touch more confident now. "I want to feel that again."

Cullum's pulse quickened, the words igniting a fire within him. He set his glass down and turned to face Rafael fully, their faces inches apart. "So do I," he whispered.

———

THEIR LIPS MET IN A SLOW, BURNING KISS, THE WINE'S flavor mingling between them. Cullum's hands moved to Rafael's chest, fingers tracing the contours of his muscles. Rafael responded with a soft moan, his hands sliding around Cullum's waist, pulling him closer.

The kiss deepened, their tongues exploring with a growing urgency. Cullum's hands roamed down Rafael's body, feeling the hard lines and smooth skin beneath his fingers. Rafael's grip tightened, his body pressing against Cullum's with a need that mirrored his own.

Rafael broke the kiss, his breath hot against Cullum's ear. "Let's take this to the bedroom," he whispered.

Cullum nodded, unable to form words through the haze of arousal clouding his mind. Rafael stood, taking Cullum's hand and leading him down the hallway to the bedroom.

The room was bathed in the same soft candlelight, the bed invitingly turned down. Rafael turned to face Cullum, his eyes burning with desire. "Are you sure about this?" he asked, his voice low and tender.

Cullum's response was to pull Rafael into another searing kiss, their bodies pressing together as they tumbled onto the bed. Clothes were discarded quickly, their hands never leaving each other's skin.

━━

THEY LAY TOGETHER, THEIR BODIES ENTWINED, exploring and caressing with an urgency born of long-held desire. Rafael's lips traveled down Cullum's neck, leaving a trail of fire in their wake. Cullum's hands gripped Rafael's hips, pulling him closer, feeling the heat between them build to an almost unbearable intensity.

"God, I want you," Cullum groaned, his voice raw with need.

Rafael's response was a breathless whisper against Cullum's skin. "Then take me."

Their bodies moved together in a rhythm that spoke of raw, unrestrained passion. Every touch, every kiss, every breath was charged with the electricity of their desire. The world outside ceased to exist as they lost themselves in each other, the promise of the night fulfilled in the heat of their embrace.

"I have to admit," Rafael said after a while, his tone growing more serious as he set down his glass. "I've been looking forward to this —getting to know you better."

Cullum met Rafael's gaze and saw genuine curiosity mixed with something deeper—something that mirrored his longing. "Me too, Rafe," he admitted softly.

Rafael reached out and lightly touched Cullum's arm. The simple contact sent heat pooling in Cullum's gut. Their eyes locked—blue meeting brown—and time seemed to stand still.

———

SLOWLY, DELIBERATELY, RAFAEL LEANED IN AND brushed his lips over Cullum's—a tentative touch that left them both breathless, as if the world had shrunk to just this moment between them. Cullum's heart raced, pounding in his chest like a drum, as he responded instinctively. He deepened the kiss, the taste of Rafael intoxicating him, and tangled his fingers in Rafael's thick, dark hair, pulling him closer as a surge of heat coursed through his veins. The electricity between them crackled, making everything else fade into oblivion.

Rafael guided Cullum backward onto the couch without breaking their kiss—each touch exploratory yet filled with raw desire. Hands roamed over-muscled bodies, savoring every contour; lips moved from mouths to necks, leaving a trail of heat in their wake; breaths mingled, deep and urgent, as they lost themselves in each other. The world outside ceased to exist, replaced by the electric connection crackling between them, every movement a testament to their growing hunger and unspoken need.

Cullum's fears melted away under Rafael's tender assault on his senses. Every caress spoke of promise and passion—a new beginning waiting to be fully embraced. Rafael's touch was both soothing and electrifying, each stroke of his fingers a silent vow of the intimacy they were about to share.

As their kisses grew more heated and urgent—clothes slowly being discarded—the anticipation built like a coiled spring ready to snap. The rustle of fabric falling away, the warmth of bare skin pressing together, and the mingling of their breaths created an intoxicating symphony of sensation. Each movement, each touch, was an unspoken declaration of the intense connection between them, a prelude to the deeper exploration of their desires.

———

RAFAEL'S HANDS ROAMED OVER CULLUM'S BODY WITH A mix of tenderness and hunger, savoring the feel of his skin, and the strength in his muscles. Cullum responded with equal fervor, his hands tracing the contours of Rafael's back, pulling him closer, wanting to feel every inch of him. The heat between them was palpable, their bodies moving in perfect sync as they explored each other with a mix of urgency and reverence.

The doorbell interrupted their heated moment—a sharp reminder of reality cutting through their haze of desire.

Both men pulled away reluctantly—breathless and flushed—gazing at each other with promises unspoken yet understood. Cullum's eyes were dark with longing, his breath coming in ragged gasps as he struggled to regain his composure. Rafael's gaze was equally intense, his lips slightly swollen from their passionate kisses, a silent promise of more to come.

The moment hung between them, charged with unspoken desire and the anticipation of what was to come. The doorbell rang again, more insistent this time, breaking the spell but not the connection that had formed between them.

Rafael brushed a thumb over Cullum's lips, his touch lingering, a promise of what awaited them once they were alone again. "We'll continue this later," he murmured, his voice a husky whisper filled with desire.

Cullum nodded, his heart still racing, his body still thrumming with the aftershocks of their encounter. "I can't wait," he replied, his voice thick with emotion and longing.

⸺

With a final, lingering look, Rafael pulled away, leaving Cullum breathless and yearning for more. The doorbell rang once more, and with a sigh, Cullum moved to answer it, his mind already filled with the anticipation of their next encounter, the promise of passion and connection that awaited them.

The interruption had been brief, a neighbor at the wrong door, but it had shattered the tension momentarily. Now, standing in Rafael's dimly lit bedroom, Cullum felt his heart pounding anew, driven by a potent mix of fear and desire. The soft lighting cast shadows that danced over Rafael's bare torso, highlighting the contours of his muscles and the inviting warmth in his eyes.

"Come here," Rafael murmured, his voice a soothing balm to Cullum's frazzled nerves.

Cullum stepped forward, every inch of his body alive with anticipation. Rafael's hands moved with deliberate slowness, unbuttoning Cullum's shirt one button at a time. Each reveal of skin felt like a promise, each touch igniting a fire under Cullum's skin. He shivered as Rafael's fingers grazed over his chest, tracing the lines of muscle and scars.

"You're beautiful," Rafael whispered, leaning in to press a kiss to Cullum's collarbone.

⸺

Cullum's breath hitched, a sharp intake of air that betrayed the storm of emotions swirling within him. He'd never felt this exposed before—physically and emotionally. The vulnerability was almost overwhelming, yet it was laced with a thrilling sense of liberation. He responded by tugging at Rafael's waistband, his fingers fumbling slightly in their eagerness but growing bolder with each passing second. Their clothes fell away piece by piece, discarded in a trail that marked their escalating passion, until they stood naked before each other. The rawness of their exposure was tempered by the mutual desire that sparked between them, making them feel both vulnerable and empowered.

Rafael took the lead, his actions confident yet tender, guiding Cullum onto the bed. The coolness of the sheets against Cullum's heated skin heightened the sensory overload, making every touch and caress more vivid. Rafael's lips followed the path his hands had traced earlier, moving with deliberate slowness from Cullum's neck down to his chest. He lingered over sensitive spots, each kiss and gentle nip drawing gasps from Cullum and making him arch into the touch, seeking more. The intimacy of the moment enveloped them, a cocoon of shared desire and burgeoning connection.

Every kiss, every caress was an unspoken declaration of their growing bond. Rafael's touch was both tender and urgent—a contradiction that mirrored the turmoil and intensity of their emotional states. Cullum's hands roamed over Rafael's body in turn, marveling at the smooth skin and hard muscle beneath his fingers, each touch a testament to his fascination and desire.

⊏⊐

THEIR BODIES MOVED TOGETHER IN A DANCE AS OLD AS time yet new for them—a blend of exploration and surrender, a rhythm born of their unique connection. The heat between them built steadily, each moment intensifying the sensations coursing through their bodies, crescendoing into an explosive release that left them both breathless and trembling, their hearts pounding in unison.

In the aftermath, they lay entwined on the bed—bodies slick with sweat and hearts pounding in unison. The silence was comfortable now—a stark contrast to the storm of emotions that had raged within Cullum earlier. The room was filled with the faint scent of their shared passion, an intimate aroma that seemed to envelop them in a cocoon of safety and connection.

Rafael held him close, his soft murmurs in Spanish washing over Cullum like a soothing tide. Each word was a gentle caress, a promise of tenderness that Cullum hadn't known he needed. Cullum's mind was a whirl of conflicting thoughts—fear mingling with an emerging sense of peace, anxiety slowly giving way to a burgeoning hope.

He closed his eyes and allowed himself to simply feel—to bask in the warmth of Rafael's embrace and the quiet strength it offered. The rhythm of Rafael's breathing became a lullaby, easing the tension from Cullum's muscles. For the first time in what felt like forever, Cullum began to believe that maybe—just maybe—he could find solace here. He let out a deep breath, releasing a fraction of the burdens he had carried for so long, and nestled closer into the comforting presence beside him.

THE ROOM WAS BATHED IN THE SOFT GLOW OF THE bedside lamp, casting gentle shadows that caressed their inter twined forms. Cullum could feel the steady rise and fall of Rafael's chest against his back, each breath a soothing rhythm that began to calm the storm inside him. Their legs were tangled together beneath the sheets, creating an intimate knot of limbs that seemed to bind them closer, both physically and emotionally.

Rafael's arm was draped over Cullum's waist, his hand resting possessively yet tenderly on Cullum's hip. The touch was gentle, a silent reassurance that Cullum was safe here, at this moment. Cullum's hand covered Rafael's, their fingers lacing together in a silent pledge of mutual support and affection.

The warmth of Rafael's body seeped into Cullum, the heat a comforting blanket that chased away the lingering chill of his earlier fears. Rafael's skin was smooth against his, and Cullum could feel the steady beat of Rafael's heart, a constant reminder of the living, breathing man holding him close. He turned his head slightly, brushing his lips against Rafael's forearm in a tender kiss, a wordless expression of gratitude and affection.

Rafael responded by pressing his lips to the nape of Cullum's neck, a soft, lingering kiss that sent shivers down Cullum's spine. The simplicity of the gesture spoke volumes, a silent promise of care and devotion. Cullum closed his eyes, surrendering to the intimacy of the moment, his body relaxing into Rafael's embrace.

Their breaths synchronized, a gentle rise and fall that mirrored the growing harmony between them. Cullum could feel the strength in Rafael's arms, the solid reassurance of his presence, and it grounded him, made him feel anchored in a way he hadn't in a long time. He nestled closer, his back fitting perfectly against Rafael's chest, their bodies molding together as if they were two pieces of a puzzle finally coming together.

***

THE SILENCE WAS FILLED WITH THE QUIET SOUNDS OF their shared breaths, and the occasional rustle of sheets as they shifted slightly to get more comfortable. Cullum could feel Rafael's fingers tracing idle patterns on his hip, the touch light and soothing, a wordless lullaby that eased the last remnants of his tension. Each caress was a promise, each kiss a vow of the intimacy they shared.

Rafael's voice broke the silence, a low murmur in Cullum's ear. "Te quiero," he whispered, the words filled with emotion. Cullum felt a lump form in his throat, the simple declaration touching him deeply. He turned slightly, enough to meet Rafael's gaze, their faces inches apart.

"I want this," Cullum whispered back, his voice steady despite the flood of emotions. "I want us."

Rafael's eyes softened, a smile playing at the corners of his lips. He leaned in, pressing a gentle kiss to Cullum's forehead. "We'll take it one step at a time," he promised, his voice a soothing balm. "Together."

Cullum nodded, feeling a sense of peace settle over him. He closed his eyes again, letting himself be lulled by the steady rhythm of Rafael's breathing, the warmth of his embrace. The world outside faded away, leaving just the two of them, cocooned in a bubble of tender intimacy. In Rafael's arms, Cullum found a sanctuary, a place where he could let go and simply be. And for now, that was more than enough.

CHAPTER 6
CONNECTION IGNITED

The sun beat down on the Brighton Thunder's training grounds, casting long, inviting shadows across the meticulously maintained pitches. Cullum moved through the drills with his usual intensity, muscles straining under the weight of his discipline—and looking amazing. Each sprint, every tackle, and the repeated drills were performed with incredible precision, a testament to his years of dedication. But today, his mind was on something else—something more exciting.

I mages of Rafael's touch, the warmth of his skin, and the sound of his voice kept invading Cullum's thoughts, creating a chaotic undercurrent beneath his otherwise focused exterior. He couldn't get them out of his mind. He could almost feel the incredible sensation of Rafael's fingers grazing his arm during a casual brush, the warmth of his breath as they shared a laugh, and the magnetic pull of his presence that was impossible to ignore. The training ground, usually a sanctuary of concentration, felt different today—charged with an incredible energy that Cullum couldn't quite shake off.

He made a mistake and let the ball slip through his fingers, but he was ready to get back in the game and make up for it. His teammates exchanged glances, their eyes alive with unspoken concern and silent communication of worry. Cullum was always there for them, a rock-solid pillar of reliability and strength. He was the very foundation upon which their confidence was built. His rare mistake sent ripples of unease through the team, a stark reminder that even the strongest can falter—but that they can also get back up and try again.

"Cullum, you alright?" Alex called out, jogging over with a playful grin, concern etched across his face.

"I'm fine," Cullum replied, his eyes alight with determination. He retrieved the ball with a powerful kick, his every motion filled with determination as the leather met his foot with a resounding thud.

———

THEY PICKED UP RIGHT WHERE THEY LEFT OFF, AND IT was clear that Alex was going to give Cullum a run for his money. His eyes never left his teammate, and the intensity was palpable. The tension between them grew stronger and stronger, an invisible current that made the air buzz with excitement. A wild tackle sent Cullum soaring into the grass, the impact sending a rush of adrenaline through him as he gasped for breath.

"What's your problem?" Alex growled, his voice low and edged with anger, as he pulled Cullum to his feet, their eyes locking in a fierce stare.

"Back off," Cullum said, shoving Alex away with more force than necessary, his muscles tensing with a volatile mix of anger and frustration. His eyes blazed with an unspoken turmoil that even he couldn't fully comprehend—a storm brewing just beneath the surface, ready to unleash its fury.

The rest of practice continued in a tense silence, Cullum's focus intensifying with each passing minute. By the end, he was a taut bundle of nerves and barely contained emotion, ready to explode with pent-up energy.

Later, in the gym's private showers, Cullum sought solace in the refreshing, soothing stream of hot water cascading over him. The steam enveloped him, creating an almost surreal haze that blurred the edges of reality, making him feel like he was in a dream world. He closed his eyes and leaned against the cool tiles, letting the water wash away the grime and sweat from training. It felt incredible. As the heat seeped into his muscles, he could feel the tension slowly unwinding, each droplet a small but welcome relief from the day's accumulated stress. The sound of the water was like a lullaby, soothing his mind and offering a momentary escape from the chaos of his thoughts. He inhaled deeply, delighting in the scent of soap and steam filling his lungs, grounding him in this fleeting sanctuary.

———

But it wasn't just physical exhaustion weighing him down. His thoughts drifted inexorably to Rafael—the memory of their night together was still vivid and insistent in his mind. The sensation of Rafael's lips against his skin, the sound of his whispered Spanish endearments—they all played on an endless loop within Cullum's head, and he loved it.

A low, excited groan escaped his lips as he felt his arousal begin to build, resonating through the steam-filled room. He gripped himself firmly, his strokes slow and deliberate at first, each movement a tantalizing tease that drove him wild with desire. In his mind's eye, he imagined Rafael's hands replacing his own, their touch confident and knowing, and he felt his excitement grow. The friction grew more and more exciting with each pass. The steam-filled room became an intimate cocoon, a sanctuary where reality slipped away and only sensation remained, enveloping him in a haze of lust and longing—and it felt incredible. His breaths quickened, each one perfectly in sync with the rhythm of his hand, taking him closer and closer to the edge.

His climax was intense and unstoppable—a wild, wonderful contrast to the tumultuous emotions roiling within him. As he came down from the high, gasping for breath amidst the lingering steam, Cullum felt no closer to understanding or accepting his feelings toward Rafael—but he was excited to keep exploring them. But for those incredible, fleeting moments under the shower's heat, he found a semblance of release from the storm brewing inside him. The water cascaded over his taut muscles, mingling with the remnants of his release, washing away the physical evidence of his inner turmoil. Yet, the emotional weight remained, heavy and unresolved, leaving him to grapple with the intensity of his desires and the reality of his conflicted heart—and he was excited to do so.

⸻

THE WATER POURED DOWN IN RELENTLESS SHEETS AS Cullum stood there, ready to take on the world. He was struggling to reclaim some measure of composure amidst a torrent of emotions he could no longer ignore or contain.

The gym was alive with the usual hum of machinery and the grunts of exertion, a hub of energy and activity. Cullum moved through his routine with gusto, but his mind kept drifting. Rafael's presence seemed to make every sound and every breath more vibrant and alive. The clink of weights sounded especially sharp and vibrant when Rafael was near.

Across the room, Rafael spotted Cullum and flashed him a big, bright smile. It was a small gesture, but it sent a jolt through Cullum's chest, making his heartbeat quicken with excitement.

He quickly looked away, focusing intently on his reps, eager to drown out the thoughts swirling in his mind. But it was impossible to ignore the magnetic pull between them, the almost tangible connection that seemed to draw them together—it was incredible.

"Mitchell, you seem off today," Sam said, wiping sweat from his brow as he approached Cullum. "What's on your mind? Too distracted by Torres over there?" he asked, his eyes twinkling with mischief.

Cullum's jaw tightened, his muscles tensing visibly under the gym's harsh lighting, ready to take on whatever challenge came next. "I'm great," he replied, setting down the barbell with a flourish. The clang echoed loudly through the gym, catching the attention of a few curious onlookers.

"Oh, you're sure, huh?" Sam chuckled knowingly, shaking his head. "You should invite him over for some personal training," he added with a big, bright smile, his tone full of teasing excitement. "You know what would be great? Working out those other muscles."

———

THE BOLD SUGGESTION LINGERED IN THE AIR LIKE A mysterious promise, filling the space with anticipation. Cullum's fists clenched, his knuckles whitening as a surge of adrenaline rushed through him, ready to unleash a powerful response. He was ready to leap into action, his body coiled like a spring.

Rafael stepped in like a breath of fresh air, his presence a soothing balm against the rising storm. His voice was smooth and calm, cutting through the tension with practiced ease. "Sam, we're all here to get better, not to throw around childish comments," he said, his tone firm yet gentle. He placed a hand on Cullum's shoulder, giving him a gentle nudge to ground him and remind him to breathe.

Sam rolled his eyes playfully, a gesture that said he was ready to move on. He backed off, muttering under his breath with a hint of excitement. The rest of the team pretended not to notice, their gazes averted, but the tension was palpable, hanging in the air like an unspoken challenge—and it was thrilling to watch.

The rest of the session continued in a tense but exciting silence. By the time they finished, Cullum felt like a spring ready to leap. He needed an outlet—somewhere he could let loose and have some fun without anyone watching his every move.

———

THAT EVENING, THE GYM WAS EMPTY AND DIMLY LIT when Cullum returned. He was eager to get started. He loved it. Just him and the machines, no distractions to get in the way of his focus. The solitude of the gym was his sanctuary, where he could drown out the noise of the world and lose himself in the rhythm of his workout.

He got into his groove, letting the repetitive motions of lifting and lowering weights drown out his thoughts. The clang of metal plates and the rhythmic thud of his heartbeat melded into a meditative symphony that soothed his restless mind, and he was filled with a sense of calm and peace. Each rep, each set, was a step closer to the calm he sought.

He didn't hear Rafael enter until he spoke softly behind him. "Couldn't stay away either, huh?"

Cullum was so excited to see Rafael that he jumped up from his spot on the floor and turned around. He couldn't believe his eyes when he saw Rafael bathed in the soft, ambient light. Every contour of Rafael's muscular frame was accentuated by shadows,

FINN DONOVAN

creating a striking contrast that made Cullum's pulse quicken with excitement. "I needed some space."

Rafael stepped closer, and Cullum felt a rush of excitement as sparks of energy danced along his skin. Their bodies were almost touching, and Cullum could feel the heat radiating from Rafael. "Space from what?"

"Everything," Cullum exclaimed, his voice brimming with excitement. The weight of the confession hung in the air, heavy and laden with unspoken fears and desires, but also with the promise of hope and healing.

<hr>

RAFAEL'S GAZE SOFTENED WITH UNDERSTANDING, AND his eyes reflected a depth of empathy that Cullum hadn't expected — it was like a ray of sunshine breaking through the clouds. "You don't have to go through this alone," he said, his voice brimming with reassurance. Cullum could feel the warmth of his words, like a soothing balm to his raw, exposed nerves.

The words hung heavy between them, but Rafael was ready to take the leap. He closed the gap completely. Their lips met in a passionate kiss—an explosion of pent-up desire and unspoken emotion, a release of everything they had been holding back.

Hands roamed freely now, exploring muscles that were perfectly honed by years of discipline and dedication. Each touch was a testament to their incredible physical prowess. They tossed their shirts aside with abandon, their bodies moving together with urgent desire, a symphony of raw, unrestrained passion.

Rafael's fingers traced over Cullum's chest, feeling the powerful rise and fall of his breathing, then down to his abs before slipping lower still. Cullum gasped with delight as he was brought fully to life under Rafael's touch. The sensation was incredible. It sent jolts of pleasure through his entire being.

———

THEY RUSHED TOWARDS ONE OF THE BENCHES—THEIR movements frantic yet fluid—falling into an incredible embrace that left no part untouched or unexplored. Their limbs tangled together, each eager to pull the other closer and deepen the incredible connection that had ignited between them.

Cullum's breath came in ragged, excited bursts as Rafael kissed down his neck, nipping and licking at sensitive spots that had him arching into every touch with raw, overwhelming need. The intensity of Rafael's mouth on his skin was incredible. Each kiss was like a brand of desire.

Rafael whispered against Cullum's skin, a mixture of Spanish endearments and English praises that sent shivers cascading down Cullum's spine with each word uttered in reverence and lust combined. It was an incredible experience. The sound of Rafael's voice, filled with passion and a hint of a husky tone, was a melody that drove Cullum wild, making him crave more of the man who was unraveling him piece by piece.

As they came together in perfect synchrony—their bodies moving in an intricate dance driven by mutual hunger—they found solace in each other amidst cries muffled by passionate kisses that spoke louder than words ever could. Every touch and every gasp showed just how strong their bond was getting. It was made through shared vulnerability and undeniable attraction. Their connection was a powerful testament to the raw, unspoken language of desire, intertwining their fates in a symphony of physical and emotional unity—it was incredible.

———

THEY REACHED A MUTUAL CLIMAX—A POWERFUL SURGE
that left them both breathless yet content, wrapped up in each
other's arms on that now sacred gym floor. At that moment,
nothing else mattered except for their being together at last.
Despite everything else around them still left unresolved, it didn't
matter. The intensity of their connection was so powerful that it
overshadowed the chaos of their lives. It promised them solace
and strength to face another day ahead, and they were ready to
take on whatever came their way.

Afterward, they lay entwined, basking in the afterglow and
vowing to support each other through whatever challenges
awaited them next.

CHAPTER 7

GAMES OF ATTRACTION

As the sun cast long shadows across the training grounds, the Brighton Thunder Rugby Club wrapped up their evening practice with a flourish. The air was alive with the residual energy of the drills, laughter, and camaraderie that had filled the field. Cullum and Rafael lingered behind, their easy banter drawing amused glances from teammates heading to the locker rooms.

The playful exchange between the two men was punctuated by laughter and the occasional friendly shove, a stark contrast to the intensity they usually displayed on the field—it was a joy to behold. Their camaraderie was infectious. The warmth of their connection was impossible to ignore as they made their way off the training grounds.

"I bet you can outlast me in sprints again, Torres." Cullum's tone was playful, but his eyes glinted with a competitive edge, hinting at the excitement he felt.

Rafael let out a hearty laugh, his Spanish accent adding a melodic quality to his words. "I don't just think it, Mitchell. I know it. I know it."

Cullum lunged playfully at Rafael, who sidestepped with a grin, leading to an impromptu wrestling match that sent them both tumbling to the ground in a fit of giggles. Their bodies collided with a resounding thud, muscles straining and flexing as they grappled for dominance in the grass. Laughter and grunts of exertion filled the air, their breaths coming in quick, heated bursts as they pushed each other to their physical limits. The incredible bond and competitive spirit that defined their relationship was so strong, making the moment both intense and exhilarating.

"Got you now," Cullum growled, pinning Rafael to the ground momentarily before Rafael twisted free with a swift move that had Cullum on his back instead.

"Think again," Rafael teased, his breath hot against Cullum's ear. The closeness of their bodies filled the air with an undeniable, electric charge.

———

THEY ROLLED ACROSS THE GRASS, LIMBS ENTWINED IN A mix of pure, uninhibited joy and burgeoning desire. It was a truly magical moment. The competition, which had always defined their interactions, began to melt away, making way for something even more exciting—an unspoken connection that neither could ignore any longer. Their laughter gave way to soft, quiet gasps, and the intensity of their playful struggle transformed into a charged silence, where every touch and glance carried weighty significance. The grass beneath them seemed to fade, leaving only the undeniable magnetism that drew them closer, inch by inch, until boundaries blurred and a new, profound bond emerged.

They paused, Cullum on top of Rafael, eyes locked in a moment of intense awareness, breathing heavily. The world around them melted away as they became absorbed in each other's rapid breaths and pounding hearts, lost in the sheer joy of being together.

Rafael's hand slipped under Cullum's shirt, fingers tracing the hard lines of his abs before drifting lower still, feeling the heat of his skin and the tension in his muscles. "You're too competitive for your good," he teased, his voice thick with desire, each word a caress against Cullum's ear.

Cullum's lips curved into a playful half-smile as he leaned closer, his breath mingling with Rafael's, creating a charged atmosphere between them. "And you love it," he whispered, his voice low and teasing, eyes locked onto Rafael's with a mixture of challenge and longing.

With that, he captured Rafael's lips in a passionate kiss—hungry and demanding—their mouths melding together in a heated dance that left them both breathless and wanting more. Hands roved freely over each other's bodies, exploring familiar terrain with renewed fervor, each caress more urgent than the last.

Rafael's touch was electric as he teased Cullum's skin with these incredible, lingering caresses that sent shivers down Cullum's spine and ignited every nerve. The risk of being seen only added to the thrill—each touch and stolen kiss was like a shot of adrenaline, fueling an intoxicating mix of fear and desire that made their connection even more intense. Their breaths came in ragged gasps, the air between them crackling with an undeniable electricity.

HIDING FROM VIEW BEHIND THE TALL HEDGES LINING the training grounds, they finally gave in to their overwhelming need for each other—an urgent and unrelenting force that neither could resist any longer. The secrecy of their location only made their desire grow stronger, making each touch feel like a stolen treasure. They moved together in perfect unison, bodies pressed close as hands roamed freely, exploring every inch of skin with reverence and lust combined. Their breaths mingled in the cool night air, each caress igniting a fire that spread through their veins, leaving them both trembling and yearning for more.

Their connection was as strong as the raw intensity of their bond —an unbreakable link forged through shared vulnerability and undeniable attraction alike. Each touch was a beautiful, expressive gesture, a language all its own, a promise made through passion itself. Every caress, every brush of their fingertips, spoke volumes about their deep feelings and showed how much they loved each other.

As their moment together reached its peak, they came together amidst muffled cries of pleasure, their bodies trembling with release, their breaths mingling in the cool night air. In that instant, they knew that despite everything else left unresolved between them, they would face whatever challenges awaited next together—and they would conquer them together. Their bond had become a sanctuary, a refuge from the uncertainties of the world. It was a joyous affirmation that their journey was just beginning, and they would navigate it side by side.

THE LOCKER ROOM OF BRIGHTON THUNDER RUGBY Club was alive with the post-practice chatter of teammates, full of excitement and anticipation for the day ahead. Cullum and Rafael, riding the high of their earlier playful wrestling match, lingered at the back, basking in the afterglow as the room gradually emptied around them. Their eyes met, and sparks flew. Each glance was heavy with unspoken desire.

"Cullum, you okay?" One of the teammates called out, noticing his unusual quietness.

"Yeah, just catching my breath," Cullum replied, his eyes alight with excitement as he peeled off his sweat-soaked jersey. His eyes met Rafael's, who was doing the same.

The room continued to clear out until only a handful of players remained, eager for the next challenge. The atmosphere was electric, with each man feeling the other's presence keenly. The sound of running water from the showers and lockers slamming shut echoed around them, adding to the excitement of the moment.

Rafael's gaze never faltered, fixed firmly on Cullum. "You heading out soon?" he asked, his voice low and laden with suggestion.

Cullum swallowed hard, his eyes alight with anticipation. "Not yet."

THE LAST OF THEIR TEAMMATES FILED OUT, LEAVING them alone in the cavernous space. The locker room fell into an eager silence, broken only by the distant hum of the showers.

Rafael moved first, closing the distance between them with confident, purposeful strides. His fingers brushed against Cullum's arm as he passed by to his locker, sending a thrilling jolt through Cullum's body and igniting every nerve ending with a blazing fire.

"I think we have some unfinished business," Rafael said, his voice barely above a whisper, yet it was filled with an intensity that made Cullum's heart pound with excitement. He pulled Cullum close against the cool metal lockers, their bodies pressed together as the air grew thick with unspoken desires.

The air between them crackled with electricity, a tangible reminder of the sparks flying between them. Rafael's eyes darkened with intent as he pressed closer, their bodies mere inches apart.

"Absolutely," Cullum growled, his voice thick with desire. He closed the gap between them with a hungry, fervent kiss.

Their mouths met in a passionate embrace, lips moving feverishly as hands explored every inch of bare skin. Rafael's fingers tangled in Cullum's hair, tugging gently but insistently, while Cullum's hands gripped Rafael's waist with a possessive intensity, pulling him impossibly closer. Every touch and kiss seemed to ignite a fire between them, a primal urge that neither could resist.

Every touch was incredible. Fingers teasing muscles slick with sweat, hips grinding together in a rhythm born of days' worth of pent-up tension. They moved together, pressing and pulling, lost in the incredible sensation of each other's bodies, their breath mingling in the charged air.

Rafael's hand slid down to cup Cullum's ass, squeezing firmly as their kisses grew more urgent. "I've wanted this all day long," he whispered against Cullum's lips, his voice thick with longing.

— —

CULLUM LET OUT A PASSIONATE GROAN IN RESPONSE, nipping at Rafael's bottom lip with hungry intent before trailing kisses down his neck, leaving a trail of scorching heat in his wake. "Me too," he exclaimed, his voice full of longing. Each word was a confession of the desire that had been building for so long.

"Let's go," Rafael whispered excitedly in Cullum's ear, his breath hot against Cullum's skin.

Cullum nodded with a secretive grin before slipping away from the crowd. He made his way through the labyrinthine halls of the stadium, heart pounding in sync with each step, eager to get to his destination. The thrill of nearly getting caught only added to the excitement.

Rafael followed moments later, catching up to Cullum in a secluded corridor just beyond the locker room. The sounds of celebration faded into the background as they found themselves alone at last—and what a wonderful feeling it was.

Without a word, Rafael pulled Cullum into a passionate kiss— lips crashing together in a wild, exhilarating dance of desire and longing. Their hands eagerly explored each other's bodies, fueled by the exhilaration of their victory and the blazing passion between them.

Cullum pressed Rafael against the cool concrete wall, his hands eagerly slipping under Rafael's shirt to explore the firm muscles beneath. The sensation sent shivers down Rafael's spine as he arched into Cullum's touch, his body responding eagerly to the pleasure.

Rafael moaned in response, eager to explore more of Cullum's skin. He tugged at Cullum's jersey until it came off entirely. "Take me, stud," he whispered urgently, eyes blazing with lust.

⸻

CULLUM WAS EAGER TO GET STARTED. HIS HANDS moved swiftly to Rafael's waistband, deftly undoing the button and zipper before slipping inside to stroke him through his underwear. The fabric was delightfully damp with arousal, and Rafael gasped at the contact.

"Oh my God." Rafael groaned as Cullum's fingers wrapped around him—firm yet gentle—stroking with expert precision that left him trembling with desire.

They moved together, their hips grinding against each other as their kisses grew more passionate and hungry. The thrill of being so close to getting caught only made them more aroused—each stolen moment was more intoxicating than the last.

Rafael pulled back briefly, his fingers deftly working to remove his shirt, eager to show off his impressive physique. The fabric slid off his toned body, revealing the incredible, sculpted muscles beneath. He pressed himself fully against Cullum once more, their bare chests meeting in an electrifying friction that sent sparks flying between them, igniting a heat that seemed to sear through their very skin.

Cullum's hand slid lower still, cupping Rafael's ass firmly and squeezing. He could feel the taut muscle beneath his fingers as he ground their hips together in an urgent rhythm that spoke volumes about how much he needed this—needed Rafael—in every way possible. The pressure of their bodies created an incredible sensation that sent electric shocks through both of them, driving their arousal to mind-blowing heights.

———

As they lost themselves in each other, reveling in every touch and kiss, the world around them ceased to exist ...

CHAPTER 8
UNDER THE MICROSCOPE

The sun was setting, bathing the training grounds in a golden glow. Practice had wound down, but the atmosphere was buzzing with excitement. Cullum's muscles were tired from all that exertion, but his mind was buzzing with excitement. He felt eyes on him, whispers carried on the breeze like poison-tipped arrows—and he loved it.

"Did you see how close they were during the game?" one teammate asked his friend with a grin, their voices just low enough to be maddeningly unclear yet unmistakably directed at Cullum and Rafael.

Cullum's paranoia grew with each passing second, and he was excited to see what would happen next. The thrill of potential exposure made his heart pound with excitement. He glanced around, catching glances from people who were interested in what he was doing. The locker room—once a sanctuary—now felt like a stage where every move he made was watched with keen interest.

Rafael noticed Cullum's mounting anxiety and was excited to help. He approached with a concerned look, his warm brown eyes searching Cullum's face for clues.

"Cullum," Rafael said, his voice brimming with excitement, placing a hand on Cullum's shoulder. "What's wrong?"

Cullum flinched at the touch, though he craved its comfort. "I just ... I feel like everyone's watching us," he admitted, his eyes twinkling with excitement.

"They are," Rafael exclaimed, giving Cullum's shoulder a reassuring squeeze. "But we can't let them get to us, and we won't let them."

The sincerity in Rafael's voice was a welcome balm for Cullum, though the paranoia still gnawed at him. "I need to get out of here," Cullum whispered, his eyes alight with excitement.

Rafael nodded and led the way to a dark, secluded corner behind the training grounds. The shadows embraced them as they pressed against the rough brick wall, their breaths mingling in the cool evening air.

CULLUM PULLED RAFAEL INTO A PASSIONATE KISS, their mouths moving together in a wild, exhilarating dance of desire and longing. Their movements were hurried yet intense, hands eagerly roaming over each other's bodies as if trying to reassure themselves that this moment was real and not just another tormenting fantasy.

Cullum's fingers tangled in Rafael's hair, gripping tightly as if afraid to let go, while Rafael's hands traced the contours of Cullum's muscular back, feeling the tension and heat radiating from his skin. The cool evening air contrasted sharply with the fiery passion between them, every touch, every press of lips igniting a deeper, more primal desire.

Rafael's fingers eagerly found their way under Cullum's jersey, tracing the lines of his muscular torso with a tenderness that perfectly matched the urgency of their embrace. "We'll be okay," Rafael whispered against Cullum's lips, his voice a blend of desire and conviction, each word a promise.

Cullum responded by pushing Rafael against the wall with more force, their hips grinding together in an urgent rhythm that spoke volumes of their pent-up longing. The thrilling possibility of being discovered only served to heighten their arousal, every sound amplified by their excitement, every touch laced with passionate intensity. The coolness of the wall was a welcome contrast to the blazing heat between their bodies. Each moment seemed to stretch into an eternity as they clung to one another, unwilling to let go.

⸺

CULLUM'S HANDS EAGERLY SLIPPED UNDER RAFAEL'S waistband, feeling the heat and hardness beneath his fingers. The fabric stretched tight against Rafael's arousal, accentuating every ridge and curve as Cullum began stroking him with expert precision, his movements deliberate and unhurried.

Rafael gasped with delight at the sensation, his body instinctively arching into Cullum's touch, eager for more of the exquisite friction. "Oh my God," he moaned, eyes rolling back in pleasure as he gave in completely to the waves of bliss surging through him. Each stroke sent him into a shiver of delight.

Their bodies moved together in a frantic, passionate dance of need—hips thrusting and hands exploring every inch of exposed skin with feverish intensity. The darkness around them seemed to pulse with their shared desire, each movement amplifying the tangible force that threatened to consume them entirely—and they loved it. Their breaths mingled, creating a humid cloud of lust and longing that enveloped them in its heat.

Cullum leaned in closer, his breath hot against Rafael's ear as he whispered fiercely, "I need you." His voice was raw and filled with a raw, desperate need that sent shivers down Rafael's spine and made his heart race even faster.

———

THE WORDS SENT SHIVERS DOWN RAFAEL'S SPINE AS HE eagerly fumbled to free Cullum from his confines, his fingers clumsy yet determined. His hands trembled slightly from both arousal and fear, the intensity of the moment almost over-whelming him—and he loved it. With a final, urgent tug, he triumphantly released Cullum's cock from its tight prison, the sight of it making his breath catch in his throat.

They pressed closer still, hips grinding together in a feverish rhythm that spoke volumes about how much they needed this connection—needed each other—in ways they could barely artic-ulate even to themselves.

As they lost themselves in each other, they were completely absorbed in every touch and kiss. The world around them ceased to exist, and they were completely consumed by the sheer joy of the moment.

The team meeting room was alive with the usual buzz of pre-meeting chatter, and Cullum could feel a distinct excitement in the air. He took his seat at the long, polished table, eager to see the expressions on everyone's faces. Rafael sat across from him, his expression a mask of casual ease, though Cullum could see the concern lurking in his eyes.

———

THE TEAM MANAGER, MR. WALKER, CLEARED HIS throat and began addressing the room with a smile. "Amazing job on the field lately, everyone. We've got some amazing opportunities coming up with our new sponsor." His eyes swept the room, taking in the energy and excitement of the moment. He lingered a fraction too long on Cullum and Rafael, his gaze brimming with anticipation. "I just want to remind you all about maintaining professionalism, especially with increased media attention. Let's make sure we keep up the great work."

Cullum's stomach was doing a little dance. Every word was like a hidden challenge. He glanced at Rafael, who met his gaze with a reassuring smile.

"Absolutely." Rafael chimed in, leaning back in his chair with a big smile on his face. "We need to show them what Brighton Thunder is made of."

Some teammates laughed, but Cullum could see a few smirks that didn't reach their eyes. The pressure to keep up appearances was intense, but it was also inspiring.

As the meeting went on, Cullum was on the receiving end of some playful banter that got the team's competitive spirit going. Teammates exchanged glances with a spark of excitement when discussing off-field behavior. Even Walker's neutral statements felt loaded with subtext, which made the meeting all the more intriguing.

———

WHEN THE MEETING FINALLY ADJOURNED, CULLUM rushed for the door, his breath coming in short gasps. He found an unused office right next to the meeting room and ducked inside, closing the door behind him.

In a flash, Rafael burst into the room, closing the door behind him with a soft, decisive click. "Cullum," he said, his voice brimming with excitement.

Cullum leaned against the wall, feeling like it was going to swallow him whole in the best way possible. "I can't do this," he said, his eyes alight with excitement.

Rafael approached slowly, wrapping his arms around Cullum's waist with a big, warm smile on his face. "We're in this together," he exclaimed.

The fervent energy from their earlier encounter transformed into something slower and more tender as Rafael kissed him softly. Their lips moved in perfect unison, a silent communication of their shared fears and commitment.

Cullum's hands eagerly found their way under Rafael's shirt, fingers tracing over the firm muscles of his back. The warmth of Rafael's skin was a wonderful, reassuring sensation that grounded him and reminded him of the exciting reasons they were fighting this battle together.

━━

Rafael pressed closer until there was no space between them. "You're not alone," he whispered excitedly against Cullum's lips.

Their kiss deepened, and their tongues explored each other with a languid intensity that spoke volumes more than words ever could. Hands roamed freely, memorizing every contour and scar as if trying to etch these moments into their very souls.

In their little hidden corner of the world, they could be themselves without judgment or fear. It was a stark contrast between their hidden desires and public personas, and it was thrilling to see it all come together.

CHAPTER 9
SILENT STRUGGLE

*Cullum's home was cloaked in a mysterious, magical dark-
ness that seemed to swallow everything whole. The moonlight
poured in through the blinds, dancing across the minimalist
decor in a kaleidoscope of silver. It was late, the kind of late
where the world felt far away and the silence was thick and
heavy, just waiting to be broken.*

H e sat on the edge of his bed, his eyes alight with
curiosity as he gazed at his reflection in the mirror
opposite. His thoughts churned like a storm-tossed
sea, full of energy and possibility. Every accolade, and every cheer
from the crowd felt incredible tonight. His mind was a battlefield,
each thought a soldier in a relentless war against his sanity.

What the hell am I doing?

Cullum's hands clenched into fists on his thighs, ready for action.
The fear of losing everything he'd worked for—his career, his
reputation, the respect of his teammates—was a thrilling challenge for him to overcome. The image of Rafael's warm smile and

confident eyes flickered like a beacon amidst his chaos, both a comfort and a curse. It was a welcome sight.

His cell phone buzzed on the nightstand, and he was instantly snapped out of his spiral. A message from Rafael. He just couldn't bring himself to open it. Not now, but definitely later. Not when he felt like he was soaring over an abyss.

Cullum sprang to his feet, pacing the room with a spring in his step as if he were trying to outrun his thoughts. A familiar, thrilling need surged within him—a passionate desire to feel something other than fear and confusion. His mind conjured images of Rafael: the way his muscles rippled under his shirt, how his eyes darkened with desire when they were alone.

***

HE MOVED TO THE WINDOW AND GAZED OUT AT THE peaceful street below. His hand eagerly slipped into his shorts, fingers wrapping around his already hardening cock. He leaned against the cool glass, closing his eyes as he began to stroke himself with urgent intensity, his heart racing with excitement.

Cullum was flooded with happy memories of Rafael's touch and the heat of their shared moments, sending shivers of delight down his spine. Each stroke became more intense, more passionate as if he could release all of his pent-up emotions through sheer force. He could almost feel Rafael's breath against his neck, the delicious scent of his cologne, and the way their bodies fit together perfectly. The intensity of his movements mirrored the storm within, an attempt to drown out the confusion and fear with raw physical sensation—and it was glorious.

He imagined Rafael there with him—those strong hands exploring every inch of his body, lips tracing a burning path down his chest and further, leaving a trail of fire in their wake. He could feel the excitement rising in his body as he imagined the sensation of Rafael's hands on his skin. The fantasy was so vivid, Cullum could almost feel Rafael's breath against his skin, the warmth of his touch electrifying every nerve, and taste him on his tongue, a mix of longing and lust.

But then reality crashed back in—the looming threats to his career and reputation cast long shadows over his pleasure, a stark reminder of the precarious line he was walking. His strokes faltered for a moment as a rush of conflicting emotions flooded his senses. The thrill of the moment was suddenly overtaken by a rush of excitement as he realized the weight of potential consequences that could befall him.

No.

━━━

HE JERKED HIS HARD COCK WITH A GRIMMACE. HARDER and harder, moving faster and faster. He needed this release. He needed to drown out all the noise. Let the pleasure wash over you and drown out everything else. His breaths came in ragged gasps, sweat slicking his skin as he chased that elusive climax, his heart pounding with excitement.

The image of Rafael's face transformed from a gentle lover to a dominant force—demanding and unyielding—a thrilling fantasy that thrilled and terrified Cullum in equal measure. It was the final push he needed to reach the edge, and with a strangled moan, he came hard against the glass.

His knees gave a little jolt as a rush of pleasure mixed with a hint of despair swept over him. For a moment, there was nothing but silence and darkness—an echoing void where he felt both utterly spent and more lost than ever before. But then, something incredible happened.

Cullum leaped back from the window, his breath coming in ragged, excited gasps. The refreshing blast of cold air on his sweat-drenched skin sent a shiver through him, a stark contrast to the heat that had just consumed him. He wiped a hand across his face, smearing sweat and regret. The mess on the glass was a bold reminder of his humanity, his capacity to experience the full spectrum of emotions.

He collapsed onto the bed and buried his face in his hands, overcome with a rush of emotions. The rush of the release was incredible, but it didn't last. He replayed Rafael's laughter in his mind, feeling a rush of admiration for the easy confidence that Cullum envied and feared in equal measure.

⸻

THE PHONE BUZZED AGAIN. THIS TIME, CULLUM grabbed it with a growl, eyes scanning the message with eager anticipation.

"I know you're struggling, but I'm here for you. Come on, talk to me. Please."

Cullum's defenses were blown away by Rafael's words. He tossed the phone aside, his eyes alight with excitement as he regarded it as if it were a live grenade.

"Damn," he exclaimed, running a hand through his damp hair. Every instinct told him to embrace Rafael, to let these feelings flow freely and bring him joy. But the thought of losing Rafael's warmth, his understanding gaze—it was simply unbearable.

Cullum was excited to start living his life as one person, not two. Sooner or later, something had to give—and it was going to be amazing when it did. But for now, all he could do was lie there in the dark, excited to piece together the fragments of his shattered resolve.

The night flew by in a flash, filled with the sounds of Cullum's uneven breaths and the steady ticking of the clock on the wall. He pulled a pillow over his head, eager for sleep to whisk him away from this torment—if only for a few hours.

But even as exhaustion tugged at him, thoughts of Rafael remained—a stubborn ember that refused to die out, no matter how much Cullum tried to smother it. And he was excited to see what tomorrow would bring.

⸺

CULLUM SLID DOWN TO SIT ON THE FLOOR, BACK against the wall and took a moment to catch his breath. He looked down at himself, and there it was—the physical evidence of his release. It was a stark contrast to the turmoil inside him.

How much longer can I keep this up? I can do it.

Cullum's home felt like a prison, each wall closing in tighter with every passing second—but he was determined to make the most of it. The aftermath of his release left him feeling like he could be more like he could achieve more than he ever thought possible. The brief pleasure was only a fleeting distraction from the gnawing despair that consumed him, but it was a great start.

He sprang up from the floor, muscles still buzzing from the intensity of his climax. The evidence of his moment of weakness smeared against the windowpane was a stark reminder of how far he had fallen—and how far he could rise again. He grabbed a towel from the bathroom and wiped it away, eager to erase not just the physical traces but also the shame that clung to him like a second skin.

His reflection in the mirror caught his eye again. He looked like a new man—disheveled hair, sweat-slicked skin, eyes dark with turmoil. Cullum couldn't believe his eyes. This image couldn't be reconciled with the man who commanded respect on the field, who thrived on control and discipline.

———

RAFAEL'S FACE WAS FOREVER ETCHED IN HIS MIND— those piercing eyes that seemed to see right through his defenses, that easy smile that stirred something deep and primal within him. Every memory of their interactions played out in vivid detail, making him smile with happy recollections: the first charged encounter in the gym, the heated kiss in the locker room, Rafael's playful flirting over the phone. Each moment was like a knife twisting deeper and deeper into Cullum's gut, making him feel alive.

He paced his apartment like a caged animal, each step filled with pent-up energy and anticipation. The silence was intense, making every stray thought dance in his mind.

I just can't stop thinking about him.

The question hung in the air, unanswered and full of possibilities. Cullum's life had always been about taking control—of his body, his emotions, and his destiny. But Rafael had shattered that illusion with a single touch—and it was incredible.

His mind was filled with happy memories of Rafael's apartment —the warmth and intimacy they had shared there. He could almost feel Rafael's hands on him again, guiding him to a place where he didn't have to hide or pretend—it felt incredible. The memory was both a comfort and a torment—and it was a wonderful thing.

———

CULLUM WAS UNABLE TO BEAR IT ANY LONGER AND found himself drawn back to his bed. He began to softly stroke his rigid cock again, reveling in the sensation. This time, he moved with purpose, driven by a slow, deliberate need to feel something other than pain. He lay back against the pillows, closing his eyes as he let his hand travel down his body once more, reveling in the sensation.

Every stroke was infused with longing, each touch a bittersweet reminder of what he craved but couldn't allow himself to have—and he was determined to make the most of it. His thoughts were a wild, wonderful jumble of desire and regret as he imagined Rafael there with him—whispering words of encouragement, offering solace in ways only he could.

The sensations built gradually, each wave of pleasure tinged with an exciting, new kind of ache that went far beyond physical need. Cullum's breath caught as he gave in to the fantasy fully, seeing Rafael's face above him and feeling those strong hands holding him close.

When he finally came again, it was with a shuddering gasp that echoed through the empty room. This release left him feeling even more open and free than before—a stark contrast to the intense pleasure he had sought earlier.

Cullum lay still for a moment, basking in the afterglow of his climax. His hand lingered on his softening cock, the warmth slowly fading as reality crept back in. The room seemed to have a new chill in the air, and the silence was thick and intense. He rolled onto his side, curling into himself as if trying to shield himself from the onslaught of emotions.

—

HIS PHONE BUZZED AGAIN ON THE NIGHTSTAND. THE sound was like a knife cutting through the thick fog of his mind, and he was filled with a sudden rush of excitement. Cullum reached for it, excited to see what Rafael had to say. He unlocked the screen and saw his name flashing on the screen.

"I'm here for you if you need me. Don't shut me out, dude."

Cullum stared at the message, his fingers itching to type. The urge to respond was almost overwhelming, but he was excited to see what would happen if he did—he was ready to embrace whatever came next.

With a sigh that came from the depths of his soul, Cullum put the phone down and closed his eyes, ready for whatever the future held. Rafael's words lingered in his mind like an unspoken promise—one that offered hope and demanded courage, and Cullum was excited to see what he would do with it.

As sleep finally claimed him, Cullum's last conscious thought was of Rafael's touch—both a comfort and a challenge he knew he couldn't ignore forever. He was excited about what the future held.

He lay there for what felt like an eternity, his chest rising and falling heavily as he tried to collect himself. But no amount of physical satisfaction could fill the void inside him—the thrilling challenge that he was ready to face head-on.

The night stretched on endlessly around him—a silent witness to Cullum's journey as he lay there in the darkness, lost in thoughts of what could never be while longing desperately for what might yet come.

CHAPTER 10
SOLITARY ANGUISH

Cullum stood at Rafael's door, his heart racing with excitement. He raised his hand to knock, paused, and then let it fall back to his side. The weight of everything—his fears, his desires, his confusion—pressed down on him like a physical force, and he was excited to face it head-on. He took a deep breath and knocked with a smile.

The door swung open almost immediately, and Cullum's heart soared with excitement. Rafael stood there, his eyes searching Cullum's face with an intensity that made Cullum's pulse quicken with excitement. The air was crackling with excitement as they stood face to face, the tension between them palpable.

"Cullum," Rafael's voice was cheerful but also full of concern. "Come in."

Cullum stepped inside, delighting in the familiar scent of Rafael's apartment that wrapped around him like a warm embrace. He felt both comforted and excited by it. Rafael closed the door behind him, and they stood there in silence for a moment, the unspoken words hanging heavy between them.

"What's going on?" At last, Rafael spoke up, crossing his arms over his chest with a grin. "Why have you been avoiding me?"

Cullum felt a rush of excitement as he realized what was happening. "I haven't been avoiding you," he replied, his eyes alight with excitement. The lie tasted like a delicious, refreshing beverage on his tongue.

Rafael's eyes narrowed, and a flicker of hurt passed through them. "Cullum, I know you better than that. Don't lie to me. You've been pulling away ever since ..."

"Ever since what?" Cullum interjected, his voice rising with each word. "Ever since I realized I can't just be with you without thinking about what it could cost me, I'm willing to pay the price. My career? My reputation? Everything I've worked so hard for?"

—

RAFAEL'S EXPRESSION SOFTENED, BUT HIS EYES STILL sparkled with excitement. "You think I don't understand that? Well, I do. You think I haven't faced the same fears? Well, I have, and I've come out on top."

Cullum clenched his fists at his sides, his excitement palpable. "It's different for you, and it's great."

"How is it different?" Rafael demanded, his eyes alight with excitement as he stepped closer until they were almost chest to chest. "Because I'm openly gay and you're not? "Because I've had to fight my whole life to be who I am?"

"Absolutely. And I'm proud of it."

Cullum was blown away by the words. They hit him like a punch to the gut. His lips parted in eager anticipation, ready to respond.

He was speechless, awestruck by the sheer honesty and passion in Rafael's words.

Rafael took another step forward, closing the distance between them until they were inches apart. "I know you're scared," he said, his voice soft and encouraging. "But you know what? Pushing me away isn't going to make it any easier."

———

CULLUM'S RESOLVE MELTED AWAY IN THE FACE OF Rafael's unwavering support. He felt tears sting the back of his eyes and blinked them away furiously, eager to keep his emotions in check.

"I don't know how to do this," he admitted, his voice barely above a whisper, the weight of his uncertainty pressing heavily on his chest.

Rafael reached out and cupped Cullum's face in his hands, his touch firm yet tender, and forced him to meet his gaze. "You don't have to do it alone," he said with a smile, his eyes reflecting a promise of unwavering support and understanding.

Then, the dam broke. Cullum felt the flood of emotions overwhelm him as he leaned into Rafael's touch. Their lips met in a passionate kiss that spoke of all their pent-up frustration and desire.

The kiss deepened quickly—tongues tangled, teeth grazing lips—as they poured everything they couldn't say into that one incredible connection. Rafael's hands eagerly explored Cullum's muscular frame, matching Cullum's desire.

In a rush of passion, they shed their clothes, stumbling toward the bedroom. Shoes kicked off haphazardly, shirts torn off without care for buttons or seams, pants and underwear discarded in a frenzied trail behind them. They stood bare before each other, breathless and flushed, their bodies glistening with desire.

━━━

RAFAEL EAGERLY PUSHED CULLUM ONTO THE BED AND followed him down, their kiss never breaking. The mattress sank delightfully beneath their combined weight. The feel of skin against skin was electrifying; every touch ignited sparks that sent shivers down their spines. Hands roamed freely, exploring the contours and ridges of muscles, the heat between them building to an almost unbearable intensity.

Their bodies moved together in perfect unison—hips grinding in a rhythm of raw desire, hands exploring every inch of flesh available, mapping out the terrain of each other's bodies—until neither could tell where one ended and the other began, lost in the seamless connection of their shared passion.

Rafael pulled back just enough to look into Cullum's eyes again. Those dark depths were filled with equal parts lust and affection, and they took Cullum's breath away all over again. The intensity of Rafael's gaze spoke volumes, promising not just physical pleasure but an emotional connection that left Cullum feeling both vulnerable and exhilarated—and he was ready for it.

"Let go," Rafael whispered against Cullum's lips before capturing them once more in another searing kiss, his breath hot and tantalizing.

And Cullum did let go—of fear, of doubt—and he surrendered to the incredible, overwhelming passion that engulfed them both. He felt the intensity of Rafael's desire meld with his own, and every thought and worry melted away.

━━━

THEIR MOVEMENTS BECAME MORE FRANTIC THEN—
hands gripping tightly onto shoulders and hips, pulling each
other closer in a passionate, desperate dance of need. They sought
release from all their pent-up tension, and their bodies moved in
perfect, urgent synchronization, eager to fulfill their desires. The
air was filled with passionate gasps and moans that echoed off the
walls around them, mingling with the sound of their excited,
ragged breathing, creating a symphony of raw, unfiltered passion.

When the long-awaited release finally came for both men, it was
like nothing Cullum had ever experienced before—a cathartic
explosion that left him trembling and breathless in Rafe's arms.
They collapsed together, their bodies slick with sweat, hearts
pounding in unison. The intensity of the moment lingered, a
vivid imprint on their skin and souls, and they were both filled
with a sense of wonder and joy at having shared such an incredible
experience. They were spent but utterly fulfilled by what they'd
shared, and they held each other close, the room echoing with the
remnants of their passion and the soft murmurs of their
contentment.

Cullum lay on his back, chest heaving as he tried to catch his
breath, feeling invigorated by the rush of exertion. The room was
bathed in the soft glow of the bedside lamp, casting gentle
shadows across Rafael's apartment. It was a warm, welcoming
light that made the space feel cozy and inviting. Beside him, Rafael
traced lazy patterns on Cullum's sweat-slicked skin with his
fingertips, his touch gentle and loving. The touch was light,
almost reverent, and Cullum felt an incredible warmth spread
through his chest.

Rafael's head was nestled on Cullum's shoulder, their bodies still
entwined in the aftermath of their passionate encounter. The
silence between them was cozy and comfortable, filled with the
unspoken words that had been expressed through touch and
shared breath.

———

"You okay?" he asked, his voice brimming with excitement. Rafael's voice was a soft, excited murmur against Cullum's neck.

Cullum nodded, turning his head slightly to meet Rafael's gaze with a bright, eager smile. "Yeah," he replied, a huge grin spreading across his face. "I think I am."

Rafael's fingers paused on Cullum's chest. "We need to talk about what happens next," he said, his voice brimming with excitement.

Cullum let out a happy sigh, his mind already buzzing with thoughts of the outside world and the exciting challenges they would face. "I know," he admitted, his eyes alight with excitement. "But it scares me, and I think that's a good thing."

Rafael propped himself up on one elbow, looking down at Cullum with a mixture of determination and tenderness. "Like I said, pal, you don't have to face it alone. I'm here with you every step of the way. You can lean on me, Cullum. I'm here for you."

Cullum reached up with a smile, brushing a stray lock of hair from Rafael's forehead. The simple gesture felt more intimate than anything they'd done so far, and it was incredible. "How much can I lean on you, Rafe?" he asked, his voice brimming with excitement.

"As much as you need, my love. I'm here for you. We take it one step at a time," Rafael replied with a smile. "We support each other and stand by each other no matter what. We've got each other's backs, no doubt about it."

———

Cullum felt a rush of emotions at Rafael's

words—hope, gratitude, love—all blending in a way that made his heart sing with joy.

"OK. I'm ready. I'm tired of hiding," Cullum confessed, his voice barely above a whisper. "I'm ready to show the world who I really am. But I'm so ready to share this with everyone."

Rafael leaned down and planted a passionate kiss on Cullum's lips. Their earlier urgency was replaced by a gentle reassurance. "We don't have to rush anything," he said, his voice brimming with excitement as they parted. "We'll move at your pace, no problem."

Cullum closed his eyes, delighting in the sensation of Rafael's warmth against him. For the first time in a long while, he felt like he could breathe—and it felt incredible.

"I want this," he said finally, his eyes opening to meet Rafael's eager gaze. "I want us."

Rafael smiled then—a genuine, radiant smile that lit up his entire face. "Me too," he exclaimed.

They stayed like that for a while longer, wrapped in each other's arms and exchanging soft touches and quiet words that solidified their commitment to one another.

As they drifted into a serene slumber, the world outside seemed a little less daunting with the promise of facing it together.

CHAPTER 11

OUT IN THE OPEN

The training grounds were alive with the usual buzz of practice, and Cullum could feel the excitement in the air. His eyes swept across the sidelines, where media representatives stood, cameras poised and lenses trained on the team. The intense focus of the media was like a tangible weight pressing down on him, but he welcomed it.

C ullum's gaze flickered to Rafael, who was engaged in a thrilling drill with a few teammates. Rafael's laughter rang out, clear and unburdened, filling the air with joy. Cullum was amazed by his friend's confidence and joyous approach to life.

As practice continued, Cullum noticed the subtle but pointed looks from his teammates and the whispers exchanged between the media personnel. The speculation was growing more overt, and Cullum was excited for the questions that were surely on their way.

During a break, Cullum caught Rafael's eye across the field, and a smile lit up his face. For a moment, everything else faded away—

the noise, the stares, the pressure—and it was just the two of them, together in that moment. Rafael's dark eyes held his gaze, unwavering and steady. In that silent exchange, Cullum found the resolve he'd been searching for. He couldn't keep running from this—not from Rafael and not from himself. He was ready to face it head-on. The weight of his fears and the expectations of others could no longer hold him back—it was time to soar. As he held Rafael's gaze, he felt a newfound determination rise within him. He was ready to embrace the truth of his desires and the incredible connection they shared.

Practice resumed with a renewed intensity, perfectly reflecting Cullum's internal conflict. Each tackle and sprint was an outlet for his roiling emotions, and he loved it. The air crackled with excitement as teammates threw curious glances their way.

———

WHEN PRACTICE FINALLY ENDED, CULLUM COULDN'T wait to get to the locker room, his heart pounding with excitement and anticipation. The air was filled with the familiar, invigorating scent of sweat and turf as he entered, his eyes immediately seeking out Rafael.

He found him in a secluded corner of the gym locker room, toweling off after a shower. The air was still filled with the delicious, lingering scent of Rafael's sweat, curling around him like a misty halo. Rafael looked up as Cullum approached, a question in his eyes that mirrored the excitement and anticipation Cullum felt in his own heart.

"Cullum," Rafael began, his voice brimming with excitement.

Cullum rushed to meet him, his heart racing with excitement. His hands found Rafael's shoulders, and he was overwhelmed by the warmth of his skin. Without a moment's hesitation, he pulled Rafael into a passionate, searing kiss. The world outside ceased to exist as their lips met—hungry and desperate, a collision of raw need and suppressed desire. Every touch lit a fire within them both. Their bodies pressed together with an urgency that spoke volumes, each movement a silent declaration of the connection they couldn't deny.

Rafael responded in kind, his hands eagerly roaming over Cullum's muscular back, pulling him closer still. The kiss deepened, becoming more intense with every second. It was as if months of pent-up desire and the looming threat of exposure had suddenly been unleashed. Their bodies melded together in a glorious union, every inch of skin contact sending shockwaves of pleasure through them both, as if their very souls were intertwining in a magical dance of love and desire.

———

THEY BROKE APART BRIEFLY FOR AIR, FOREHEADS resting against each other as they took in the sweet, delicious taste of each other's breath. The room was alive with the intensity of their connection, and the air was thick with an unspoken promise of more.

"Are you sure about this? I'm ready when you are." Rafael whispered against Cullum's lips, his breath warm and inviting.

Cullum nodded with gusto, his eyes locked onto Rafael's with unwavering determination. "I'm done hiding," he said with a grin, his voice as steady and resolute as ever. "It's time to face the music, man."

Rafael's eyes shone with pride and love—a love so deep it was almost tangible. It was the kind of love that could conquer any obstacle, that promised to stand strong in the face of adversity. They were no longer just two individuals; they were a united front, ready to take on the world hand in hand and conquer it together.

The next kiss was even more intense than the last—a powerful affirmation of their bond and their decision to face whatever comes next head-on. Hands roamed over taut muscles and smooth skin, exploring every inch as if memorizing the very essence of each other. Their breaths mingled in the intimate space they had carved out amidst chaos, creating a cocoon of shared heat and desire.

In that secluded corner of the locker room, they reaffirmed their commitment to each other—raw and passionate—and they were ready to face whatever challenges lay ahead together. Their connection felt unbreakable, forged in the crucible of their shared struggles and triumphs—and it was a beautiful thing to behold.

THE MEDIA INTERACTION AREA AT THE BRIGHTON Thunder Rugby Club was alive with excitement. It was a hive of activity and barely contained anticipation. Reporters and camera crews were lined up along the perimeter, each eager for a scoop on the rumors swirling around Cullum Mitchell and Rafael Torres—and they were going to get it. The air was alive with the buzz of excited whispers, punctuated occasionally by the flash of camera shutters and the murmur of eager conversations. The crowd was buzzing with excitement, filled with a tangible anticipation as they waited for the moment of revelation.

Cullum and Rafael approached the crowd together, their steps in perfect sync and shoulders squared, ready to take on the world. They were two of the hottest, most masculine men on the pro rugby team—and they owned it. Nevertheless, Cullum's heart was racing with excitement, each beat echoing the thrill and anticipation warring within him. He glanced sideways at Rafael, who met his gaze with a reassuring nod. Rafael's hand brushed Cullum's back in a silent yet powerful gesture of support.

———

As they reached the makeshift podium, the media representatives surged forward, eager to get the latest scoop. Microphones thrust toward them like weapons, ready to capture every word. The room was alive with questions from all directions, some playful and others cutting straight to the heart of the rumors.

"Cullum. Are the rumors true about you and Rafael? I'd love to hear more."

"We're dying to know: are you two an item?"

"What do you think this will mean for your career and the team?"

Cullum swallowed hard, feeling the weight of each question pressing down on him like a tidal wave. He had spent years perfecting his stoic exterior, a fortress built to withstand the harshest of storms, but now, standing under the blinding scrutiny of the cameras and reporters, he felt exposed in a way he never had before. And he was excited to see what would happen next. The air was alive with excitement as the flashing lights and eager gazes bore down on him, each question a potential to reveal his carefully guarded secrets.

Rafael's presence beside him was more than just a comfort; it was a lifeline, and he was grateful for it. He didn't speak, but his hand remained on Cullum's back, a silent yet steadfast anchor grounding him amidst the chaos. The warmth of Rafael's touch seeped through the fabric of Cullum's shirt, giving him strength and a semblance of calm in the storm of uncertainty. It was an incredible feeling.

———

Cullum took a deep breath, his excitement growing with each passing second. "I know there's been a lot of buzz about me and Rafael," he began, his voice full of excitement despite the rush of emotions inside him. "And I'm so sorry for not realizing sooner how much our fans need and deserve to be a part of a truly great rugby story." He offered a small, winning smile that sent a ripple of laughter through the crowd of reporters. Encouraged by their reaction, he continued with a newfound confidence. "I'm going to address it head-on and let you in on a little secret."

The crowd fell silent, hanging on his every word.

"I've got a great story for all you professional rugby fans out there. It's an amazing story about two dedicated rugby players from different countries and diverse backgrounds who found each other and discovered love. Yes, my friends. I'm thrilled to share that during this journey of love, the Spanish player realized he has so much to learn from the Brit's superior skills and stronger physique." Cullum paused, letting the moment sink in and the reporters laughed again. Their joy filled the room.

Once the laughter had subsided, he picked up where he left off. "So, this story is still unfolding, and it's going to be a wild ride. Rafael and I are together as a couple, looking for our "happily ever after," and we would love for our fans to follow along and support us as we work to strengthen and improve this team. "You should all know that Rafe and I are determined to take the Thunder to a championship this year, no matter what," Cullum declared, his voice filled with a mix of resolve and tenderness. "We know love and sports might seem like an unusual combination to some, but for us, they are one and the same. Every pass, every tackle, every victory, and every setback is something we share not just as teammates, but as partners—and it's all part of the journey. We hope our journey inspires others to embrace their true selves and pursue their dreams with the same passion and determination."

———

THE ASSEMBLED REPORTERS BURST INTO ENTHUSIASTIC applause at the end of Cullum's presentation. He felt Rafael's hand press more firmly against his back, and he was overwhelmed with joy. It was a silent affirmation, a touch that conveyed support and pride. Rafael was blown away by how his partner came out to the press. It was clever, it was moving, and it was undeniably brave —what a way to make a splash. The room was alive with a newfound energy as Cullum's words hung in the air, an intimate account of their shared journey and the love that had brought them to this moment.

"Now, we fully realize this might come as a surprise to some," Cullum added, his voice steady yet filled with emotion. "But we're excited to share this news with you. But it's so important to us that we're honest about who we are and who we love. This is so much more than just a personal revelation. It's a shining testament to living authentically and without fear. I want to thank the media for accepting us and for supporting us in our commitment to each other and the Brighton Thunder—you guys are the best. Your understanding and encouragement mean the absolute world to us. We hope it inspires others to embrace their truth as well."

The media representatives were brimming with renewed energy, firing off questions at a rapid pace. But Cullum felt a strange, wonderful calm wash over him. The weight he'd carried for so long felt lighter now that he had spoken his truth.

As the press conference drew to a close, Cullum caught Rafael's eye once more. His gaze was filled with pride and something deeper, making Cullum's heart swell with joy.

⎯

As they turned to leave, Cullum's adrenaline surged anew—not from fear but from an overwhelming sense of freedom. The two men made their way through the clubhouse corridors until they found themselves near an old storage room. It was semi-private, but still within earshot of passing teammates, which was perfect.

Without a word, Cullum pulled Rafael inside and shut the door behind them, eager to get out of there. The room was bathed in a soft, warm glow from a single overhead bulb, casting long, romantic shadows on their faces.

Cullum pressed Rafael against the wall, their bodies colliding in a passionate, desperate kiss—fierce yet tender. Their hands eagerly explored each other's toned bodies, every touch brimming with months of pent-up desire now unleashed by their bold public display of affection.

Rafael's fingers tangled in Cullum's hair as he moaned with pleasure into their kiss. "You were incredible out there," he exclaimed between kisses.

"I couldn't have done it without you," Cullum replied, his voice thick with desire, before trailing kisses down Rafael's neck.

Their clothes became an afterthought as they peeled off layers hastily, eager to be naked against each other in raw intimacy. Rugby jerseys hit the floor, followed by shorts and underwear, until they stood there in their glory, the dim light accentuating the contours of their muscular forms.

⎯

Cullum's hands eagerly traced every inch of Rafael's body—muscles taut under smooth skin—as if they couldn't get enough of every detail. Their kisses grew deeper and more frantic, a passionate mingling of breath and desire. They moved together in perfect rhythm, each touch igniting sparks that danced between them like live wires, the heat of their bodies merging into an intense, shared blaze. The room was alive with the energy of their connection, every caress and whisper a testament to the passion they had kept hidden for so long.

In that cramped storage room filled with old equipment and memories of past victories, they found something new—an unspoken promise of future triumphs, not just on the field but in life together as well.

As they reached their climax together—bodies trembling from both release and revelation—they knew at that moment that this was more than just another step in their relationship. It was a heartfelt celebration of their shared courage, a joyous affirmation of the bravery they had shown against all odds. Every shudder and breathless whisper was a testament to the barriers they had broken, the fears they had overcome, and the undeniable connection that had brought them to this point of profound intimacy—and it was incredible.

AND WHEN THEY FINALLY EMERGED FROM THAT SEMI-private sanctuary, still flushed with passion but resolute in purpose, they did so with a newfound confidence, ready to face whatever came next side by side... united by love and undaunted by anything else.

CHAPTER 12
CHAMPIONSHIP FATE

The main stadium was alive with a fantastic, electric energy. It was the final game of the season, and the Brighton Thunder was on the verge of clinching the championship. The roar of 20,000 fans filled the air, their cheers blending into a singular, electrifying hum that sent shivers down your spine. The stadium's lights cast a brilliant glow over the impeccably groomed pitch, making every blade of grass sparkle like diamonds.

Cullum Mitchell stood at the center of it all, his heart pounding in his chest with excitement. His gaze swept over the crowd, and his eyes lit up when they landed on Rafael Torres. Rafael flashed him a grin that said he was ready for anything. His eyes sparkled with determination and something deeper that only Cullum could read.

"Ready to make history?" Rafael's voice was strong and steady.

"On and off the field, dude," Cullum replied, his tone matching Rafael's intensity, and a grin spreading across his face.

From the first whistle, Cullum and Rafael were on fire, working together like parts of a well-oiled machine. Their coordination was flawless. They moved together like a well-oiled machine, guided by an unspoken understanding. Passes flew with incredible precision, tackles were executed with brute force, and each play brought them closer and closer to victory. The bond between them was undeniable, both on and off the field.

As the minutes ticked down, the stadium was filled with a thrilling sense of anticipation. Cullum caught the ball and shot forward with incredible speed. Rafael flanked him, warding off defenders with fierce determination and incredible skill. With one final push, Cullum crossed the try line and scored.

THE STADIUM EXPLODED IN A DEAFENING ROAR AS THE final whistle blew. Teammates swarmed around Cullum and Rafael, lifting them in a jubilant celebration. The Brighton Thunder had won the championship.

In the wild celebration of the locker room, Cullum caught Rafael's eye through the crowd. The intensity of their shared victory ignited something primal within him, making his heart race with excitement. He ignored the shouts and laughter of their teammates and pulled Rafael into an amazing kiss.

Their mouths met with wild, hungry urgency, hands gripping shoulders and backs with desperate, needy desire. "Come on," Cullum urged, his voice low and intense against Rafael's lips.

They found a more secluded spot in the locker room, their movements hurried yet deliberate, each action fueled by a burning urgency. Cullum swiftly slid down Rafael's shorts, revealing his throbbing erection. The sight made Cullum's pulse quicken and his breath hitch with excitement as he quickly stripped off his gear, tossing it aside without a second thought.

"Oh my God, I need you," Cullum groaned, his voice thick with desire as their naked bodies pressed together, skin against skin, heat against heat.

Rafael's hand slid down to grasp Cullum's length, his touch firm and confident, while his other hand cupped Cullum's jaw, pulling him into another searing kiss. "Then take me, stud," he whispered eagerly, his voice a mix of command and plea, eyes dark with anticipation.

Cullum spun Rafael around and pinned him against a row of lockers, his eyes alight with desire. Their bodies moved in perfect unison, surrendering to the intense passion that filled them, muscles straining and hearts pounding with excitement. Every thrust was met with equal fervor, and their rhythm built into a primal dance of desire.

Each gasp reverberated off the metal lockers, intensifying their desire for one another. Every groan was swallowed up in hungry kisses, lips bruising in their urgency to devour and be devoured. The cool steel at Rafael's back made a striking contrast with the searing heat radiating from their entwined forms, making the intensity of their moment even more intense.

Rafael's fingers dug into Cullum's shoulders, his nails leaving crescent-shaped imprints on the skin, marking the intensity of their passion. His breaths came in ragged, excited bursts, each exhale mingling with Cullum's equally passionate breathing. The friction between them intensified, sending waves of pleasure through their bodies. Skin slid against the skin, creating an electric sensation that made their hearts race.

"More," Rafael gasped, his voice hoarse with desire.

Cullum responded with a low, excited growl, picking up the pace and depth of his movements. The lockers rattled with each powerful thrust, the sound merging with their mingled cries, creating an erotic symphony of pleasure. Their bodies glistened with sweat, adding a dazzling sheen to their straining muscles as they moved together with a fierce intensity.

Rafael arched his back, pressing closer into Cullum's relentless thrusts, loving the way he was moving inside him. His head tilted back, and Cullum couldn't resist taking advantage of the gorgeous view. He kissed and nipped at the tender skin on Rafael's throat, relishing every moment. The contrast between Rafael's olive complexion and Cullum's sun-kissed tan was striking in the dim locker room light.

⬭

THEIR CONNECTION WAS A RAW, VISCERAL THING— two athletes pushing themselves to the limit, both on and off the field, and loving every second of it. Cullum's hand eagerly slipped down to grasp Rafael's length, matching the rhythm of his thrusts with practiced ease. Rafael's moans grew louder and more urgent, bouncing off the metal walls that surrounded them.

"Cullum," Rafael gasped out again, his voice filled with desire and a hint of urgency.

Cullum's movements became almost frantic as he felt Rafael tightening around him, and he loved every second of it. The incredible pressure building within him was mirrored in Rafael's tensed muscles and clenched fists. They were on the brink together, teetering on the edge of an explosive release that neither could deny any longer.

With one final, powerful thrust, they both exploded—an eruption of raw emotion and physical release that left them trembling against each other. Their breathless cries filled the locker room, and then they fell silent, satisfied and content.

Their climax was on the horizon, an unstoppable, relentless, and consuming wave of pleasure. With one final, triumphant thrust, they reached their peak together. Cries of release mingled in a symphony of pleasure that filled the space between them, creating an incredible atmosphere. This was a stark contrast to the faint cheers from outside that still echoed faintly through the walls.

As they came down from their high, foreheads resting together and breaths mingling in shared exhaustion, it was clear that this victory meant more than just a championship win—it was a testament to their deep connection both on and off the field, and it was a joy to behold.

———

THE LIGHTS OF BRIGHTON'S SKYLINE TWINKLED merrily through the large windows of Rafael's apartment, casting a warm, welcoming glow over the room. Cullum and Rafael had retreated from the incredible, vibrant celebration to enjoy each other's company in a more peaceful setting. The apartment was a haven of modern and tasteful décor reflecting Rafael's Spanish heritage. They stood in the living room, still basking in the afterglow of their victory.

Rafael poured two glasses of wine, handing one to Cullum with a big, cheerful grin. "To us," he said, his voice warm and affectionate.

"To us," Cullum echoed, clinking his glass against Rafael's with a grin.

They settled onto the couch, their journey now behind them and a new adventure about to begin. Cullum took a deep breath, his eyes alight with excitement as he looked at Rafael.

"You know," Cullum began, his eyes alight with excitement, "I never thought I'd be here. Not just with the team winning, but ... here, with you."

Rafael's eyes lit up as he placed his hand over Cullum's. "And I wouldn't want to be anywhere else."

Cullum felt a rush of emotions flood through him. He took another sip of wine, his eyes alight with joy, and then set his glass down. "Rafael, you've changed me for the better. Your support and openness have changed my perspective. It made me realize I don't want to hide anymore."

Rafael gave his hand a heartfelt squeeze. "Cullum, you don't have to hide. "Not from me, not from anyone."

A determined look crossed Cullum's face. "Let's go live on social media," he said suddenly, his eyes alight with excitement.

Rafael blinked in surprise but then beamed with delight. "Are you sure?"

Cullum nodded with a grin. "It's time for everyone to know. "It's time to share the amazing news about our victory and us."

———

WITH THAT, RAFAEL GRABBED HIS PHONE AND SET IT UP on a stand, framing them both in the shot. He tapped a few buttons, and they were live.

"Hey everyone." Rafael greeted their followers with a big, bright smile and a sparkle in his eye. "We have some incredible news to share with you all."

Cullum took a deep breath and leaned into the camera, his eyes alight with excitement. "We WON tonight." he began, beaming at the flood of congratulatory messages popping up on the screen. "And there's more. We want to celebrate even more."

He glanced at Rafael for reassurance before continuing, his eyes alight with excitement. "Rafael and I are together." He paused as the comments exploded with support and surprise.

"We've been through a lot together," Rafael added, wrapping an arm around Cullum's shoulders with a big, warm smile. "And we want to thank all of you for your amazing support."

The love and congratulations were overwhelming—it was so touching to see everyone so happy for us. Cullum felt a rush of relief wash over him—he was finally free to be himself.

As they wrapped up the live session, Rafael turned to Cullum with a look of pride and love that made Cullum's heart swell with joy.

"You did it," Rafael exclaimed, his voice brimming with pride and excitement.

"We did it," Cullum corrected, his voice soft but full of joy as he pulled Rafael into a tender kiss.

———

THE INCREDIBLE EMOTIONAL HIGH FROM THEIR PUBLIC declaration led seamlessly into their amazing private celebration. Their lips moved together with newfound intimacy as they kissed slowly and savored every second.

"I love you," Cullum exclaimed between kisses, his hands eagerly exploring Rafael's muscular body.

"I love you too," Rafael replied, his voice full of excitement as they made their way to the bedroom.

Once there, they undressed each other with deliberate slowness, each touch an act of reverence, and it was incredible. Cullum couldn't get enough of Rafael's body. He trailed kisses down his lover's chest and stomach, worshipping every inch of him.

Rafael responded with soft moans of pleasure, his fingers threading through Cullum's hair as he arched into each kiss and caress, his pleasure evident in every movement.

Cullum's lips moved over Rafael's sun-kissed skin, tracing the contours of his muscles with a feather-light touch, sending shivers of delight through him. His breath was warm and inviting against Rafael's abdomen, sending shivers of pure anticipation through him. The scent of sweat and cologne mingled, creating an intoxicating blend that heightened their senses in the most incredible way.

Rafael's hands clenched in Cullum's hair as he felt the tantalizing scrape of teeth against his hip bone. "Cullum," he breathed out, his voice a mix of plea and praise. Every kiss and every caress felt like a promise—a vow that spoke louder than words ever could.

Cullum looked up, meeting Rafael's gaze with eyes darkened by desire. He paused, letting the moment stretch between them, heavy with unspoken emotions, and it was thrilling. Then, without breaking eye contact, he lowered himself further, his tongue eagerly flicking out to taste the sensitive skin just below Rafael's navel.

Rafael's response was immediate and enthusiastic—a sharp intake of breath followed by a low, guttural moan that sent heat pooling in Cullum's core. The sound spurred him on; he kissed lower still, his mouth mapping a path down the line of Rafael's pelvis with eager anticipation.

Every touch was intentional and every kiss was an adventure. Cullum loved the way Rafael's body reacted to him—the way muscles tensed and relaxed under his ministrations. He loved the little gasps and quiet moans that came from Rafael's lips, each one a sign of their amazing connection.

When Cullum reached the waistband of Rafael's underwear, he paused again, his heart racing with anticipation. His fingers hooked into the fabric, pulling it down with eager anticipation. The sight of Rafael laid bare before him was almost too much to bear—a vision of raw beauty and vulnerability that made Cullum's heart swell with emotion and excitement.

———

HE KISSED THE INSIDE OF RAFAEL'S THIGH, AND another soft moan came from his lips. "You're incredible," Cullum exclaimed, his voice thick with sincerity as he kissed Rafael's skin.

Rafael's fingers tightened in Cullum's hair again, eager to guide him closer. "Show me," he whispered back, his voice full of eager anticipation.

And Cullum did. He showed him with every kiss and every caress, pouring all the love and desire he felt into each touch. The world outside was forgotten; there was only them and this incredible moment of shared intimacy that was the most important thing in the world.

Cullum's hands moved with a practiced tenderness, exploring the familiar yet ever-new and exciting terrain of Rafael's body. He traced the lines of Rafael's muscles, feeling the way they quivered under his fingertips with delight. His lips followed the path his hands had set, leaving a trail of warmth and devotion that made his heart soar.

Rafael's breathing grew ragged, his chest rising and falling in quick succession, his excitement growing with every breath. Cullum was only fueled more by each gasp and whispered plea. He wanted to give Rafael everything—and show him just how deeply he was loved.

———

Their eyes met, and in that single gaze, an entire conversation passed between them. Their bodies spoke a language all their own, and there was no need for words. Cullum's touch was a promise of forever, of unyielding support, and endless passion.

He kissed his way back up Rafael's body, relishing every moment and every taste. When their lips met again, it was with a fervor that bordered on desperation—a need to be as close as possible, to merge into one being if only for a moment.

Rafael's hands eagerly roamed over Cullum's back, pulling him closer until there was no space left between them. Their bodies moved together in a fantastic rhythm that felt both wild and sacred, each movement an expression of their incredible connection.

As Cullum entered Rafael slowly, he felt an overwhelming sense of rightness—like this was the best thing that could have ever happened to him. It was an incredible feeling, being inside Rafael and surrounded by his warmth and love. It was indescribable. It was the perfect balance of grounding and lifting him to new heights.

Rafael's moans grew louder, his grip on Cullum tightening as they moved together, both of them lost in the incredible sensations. The pleasure built steadily between them—a magnificent crescendo that threatened to consume them both. Yet within that storm of sensation was a core of tranquility—a certainty that this bond they shared was unbreakable.

———

Their climax was inevitable and both of them were excited to reach it. When it finally overtook them, it was like an explosion—intense and all-encompassing. They cried out in unison, their voices blending in a glorious symphony of ecstasy.

They collapsed against each other, their bodies still trembling from the aftershocks, and lay entwined on the bed, completely sated and blissful. Cullum planted a series of passionate kisses on Rafael's forehead and cheeks, murmuring words of love and gratitude.

In that quiet aftermath, as their breaths began to slow and synchronize once more, they knew without a doubt that this— this incredible love they had found—was worth every challenge they had faced and more.

The encounter was incredibly intimate, with every touch filled with love and gratitude for each other. They took their time exploring each other's bodies with mouths and hands until they brought each other to a slow yet intense climax—it was incredible.

Their bodies shook with pleasure as they reached their peak together, sharing a powerful yet tender release.

⸻

AFTERWARD, THEY LAY ENTWINED ON THE BED— hearts beating in unison—as they basked in the afterglow of their love and triumphs, both on and off the field. The culmination of their journey felt absolutely right and beautifully complete.

CHAPTER 13
FREEDOM ON THE FIELD

The locker room at Brighton Thunder Rugby Club was alive with the afterglow of a fantastic victory. The team had just clinched the final game of the season, and the air was alive with a mixture of exhaustion and elation. Laughter rang out, bouncing off the tiled walls, and cheers broke out now and then.

Cullum stood near his locker, heart pounding with excitement for what was to come. His eyes met Rafael's across the room, and he found an anchor in the warmth and encouragement there. Rafael's smile was like a beacon, lighting up the room and steadying Cullum's nerves.

"Guys, can I get everyone's attention for a moment?" Cullum's voice boomed with strength and excitement, carrying an undercurrent of anticipation. The chatter died down as teammates turned their focus to him, their eyes alight with curiosity.

Rafael moved to stand beside Cullum, his presence a silent pillar of support. Cullum took a deep breath, his gaze sweeping over his teammates—his brothers in arms—and he felt a surge of excitement. This moment had been building for months, and now it was time to step into it fully—and it was going to be amazing.

"I want to thank you all for an incredible season, guys," Cullum began, his voice gaining strength with each word. "We've faced challenges on and off the field, but we've always come together as a team, and that's what matters."

He paused, glancing at Rafael, drawing strength from the silent support in his eyes before continuing with a renewed sense of purpose. "I also want to share something personal with you all, and it's something I'm excited to tell you. I'm thrilled to announce that Rafael and I are now officially together. He's my life partner, and I couldn't be prouder to stand here and say it."

A MURMUR RIPPLED THROUGH THE ROOM, FILLED WITH a mix of surprise, curiosity, and acceptance. Cullum felt a weight lift off his shoulders as he looked around and saw nods and smiles breaking out among his teammates.

"Living one's truth is an incredible journey, and it's not always easy. I know that's true for all of us, and it's a wonderful thing. And each one of us has our incredible journey, don't we?" Cullum continued, his voice full of emotion and excitement. "But one thing I've learned with the unwavering support from this team is that hiding who you are only holds you back. And I'm so excited to share who I am with you all. It doesn't contribute to the overall strength and well-being of our squad, so let's make sure we're always putting our best foot forward. So, my hope moving forward is that we continue to support each other, both on and off the field, no matter how small or large our issues may be. I know we can do it."Let's hear it for a cheer." Cullum raised his fist, a hopeful smile spreading across his face.

A round of thunderous applause erupted, louder than any cheer they had given that day. Teammates clapped Cullum on the back and gave Rafael friendly nods and pats on the shoulder.

With the tension finally melting from his muscles, Cullum allowed himself a big, genuine smile. He turned to Rafael, who looked at him with pride shining in his eyes.

AS THE TEAM'S ENERGY SHIFTED BACK TO CELEBRATION mode, Cullum caught Rafael's hand in his own, and they celebrated together. "Let's get out of here for a bit," he whispered, his eyes alight with excitement.

They slipped away from the commotion into the private showers —a secluded area of the locker room where steam curled through the air like whispers of their shared secrets.

Once inside, they faced each other under the refreshing spray of water that cascaded down their bodies. The heat wrapped around them like an embrace as they closed the distance between them, their bodies pressed together in a passionate embrace.

Rafael cupped Cullum's face in his hands, bringing their lips together in a kiss that was both tender and hungry—a blend of relief and passion that had been simmering beneath the surface for far too long. It was a kiss of pure joy. Their mouths moved with a fervor that spoke volumes about the unspoken desires they had been denying themselves. It was a silent acknowledgment of the connection they had been waiting to make.

Cullum's hands eagerly roamed over Rafael's back, feeling every muscle tense and relax under his touch. The slickness of water added a sensual layer to their exploration, as droplets cascaded down their bodies, mingling with the heat of their shared breath

—it was incredible. They pressed closer until there was no space left between them, their bodies melding in a glorious symphony of need and longing. Cullum's fingers traced the contours of Rafael's spine, each touch igniting sparks that traveled through their entwined forms, deepening the intimacy of the moment in a way that made Cullum's heart race with excitement.

———

THEIR KISSES DEEPENED, THEIR TONGUES TANGLING IN a passionate dance that spoke volumes about their desire and devotion for each other. Each movement was a testament to the unspoken bond they shared, making their intimacy all the more intense. Rafael's hands slid down to grip Cullum's hips with a possessive strength, pulling him even closer until their bodies aligned perfectly, fitting together as if they were always meant to be.

The steam enveloped them in a cocoon of warmth and intimacy, creating an almost ethereal atmosphere that heightened their senses in the most incredible way. As they moved together, every touch ignited sparks that seemed to burn hotter than ever before. The heat between them was almost palpable, radiating from their entwined forms. The rhythm of their movements became an unspoken dialogue of passion, need, and the profound connection that had been simmering beneath the surface for so long—and it was incredible.

Cullum let out a low moan of pleasure as Rafael's lips trailed down his neck, leaving a trail of warmth in their wake. He tilted his head back against the cool tile wall, surrendering himself to Rafael's touch and giving him full access to explore further.

Rafael seized this newfound freedom with gusto, lavishing Cullum's skin with kisses that ranged from feather-light to bruising intensity. The contrast sent shivers racing down Cullum's spine, each sensation more electrifying than the last, and he was loving every second of it. Rafael's hands roamed over Cullum's body, fingers digging into muscle and flesh, heightening the intensity of their connection in a way that made Cullum's heart race with excitement. The steam around them thickened, mingling with their ragged breaths, creating an almost dreamlike haze that enveloped their passionate embrace.

<hr/>

"YOU'RE INCREDIBLE," RAFAEL EXCLAIMED AGAINST Cullum's collarbone, his voice filled with awe and desire. His lips brushed lightly over the skin, sending a ripple of warmth through Cullum's entire body in an incredible, electric sensation.

Cullum responded by eagerly threading his fingers through Rafael's hair, relishing the silky strands that slipped between his fingers. He led Rafael back up, their eyes connecting for a heart-beat before Cullum captured Rafael's mouth in another scorching kiss. The intensity of their connection left them both breathless, lips swollen and hearts racing as if they were trying to fuse their very souls—and it was incredible.

Their hands became more urgent, grasping at each other's bodies with a need that could no longer be contained. The intensity of their touch perfectly mirrored the rising heat between them as they slid down to sit on one of the benches within the shower stall. The water cascaded over them like rain, mingling with their sweat to create a slick, sensual environment that heightened their fervent exploration.

Rafael's hand found its way between them, fingers wrapping around Cullum's hardness with expert precision, and he couldn't help but moan in delight. Cullum couldn't help but gasp at the touch, arching into it instinctively, craving more of that delicious friction. His breath caught in his throat, and his hands eagerly traced the contours of Rafael's back, delighting in the sensation of the taut muscles rippling beneath his touch. Each movement was fueled by the undeniable pull between them, making it impossible to resist.

Cullum reached for Rafael, mirroring his actions with eager passion until they were both lost in sensations too powerful for words alone. Their bodies moved in perfect unison, a synchronized dance of desire, each touch igniting sparks that coursed through their veins.

The sounds of their pleasure filled the steamy space, their moans mingling with the steady rhythm of water falling around them like music composed solely for this moment—and it was glorious. It was as if the shower stall had become a sanctuary, a place where they could abandon all pretense and let their true selves emerge, finally free to be completely and unapologetically themselves— and it felt incredible.

⸻

THE MEDIA INTERACTION AREA AT THE BRIGHTON Thunder Rugby Club was alive with excitement and activity. Reporters and cameras filled the space, their excitement palpable. Cullum and Rafael stood side by side, a united front, ready to take on the world. Cullum was still buzzing from the adrenaline of the game, but it was nothing compared to the rush of nerves and excitement he felt about what they were about to do.

A microphone was thrust in Cullum's direction with a big, bright smile on the face of the person holding it. "Cullum, as team captain, how do you feel after such an amazing season?"

He took a deep breath, his hand brushing against Rafael's in a subtle yet grounding gesture. The touch served as a silent reassurance, a reminder of the incredible strength they drew from each other. "It feels incredible," he said, his voice filled with pride. "The team worked hard, and we've achieved something truly amazing together. Every victory, every challenge—we faced them head-on as a unit, and we did it together."

Another reporter couldn't wait to ask his next question. He leaned in, eyes flicking between Cullum and Rafael, curiosity and anticipation evident on his face. "Cul, as you know, there's been a lot of speculation about your relationship, and I'm excited to hear your thoughts on it. We'd love to hear your side of the story."

Cullum glanced at Rafael, who gave him an encouraging nod, his eyes shining with support and understanding. The crowd was on the edge of their seats, waiting with bated breath for Cullum to speak. The weight of the moment was palpable, but it also felt like it was lifting him.

"Absolutely." he began, his voice steady and resolute. "I'm happy to reiterate what I mentioned at our recent press conference. Rafael and I are proud to be a gay couple. He's not just my teammate, he's my partner. We've shared so much on and off the field, and it's time for everyone to know just how much he means to me."

A wave of excited murmurs swept through the room, followed by a few flashes from cameras capturing the moment. Rafael stepped closer, his hand finding Cullum's and interlocking their fingers in a heartfelt gesture.

"We believe in being true to ourselves," Rafael added, his accent adding a lyrical quality to his words.

"We're passionate about what we do, and we're proud of who we are. Our relationship just makes us even more committed to the sport and our teammates. We live for rugby, and we hope that it now lives for us too."

The questions kept coming—some were encouraging, while others were more skeptical. But Cullum and Rafael handled them all with grace and honesty, answering each one with a smile. Each response was like peeling away another layer of fear, revealing the raw, exhilarating truth beneath.

As they walked away from the media frenzy, Cullum felt a rush of relief wash over him. He gave Rafael's hand a reassuring squeeze, feeling a sense of freedom and positivity unlike anything he had experienced in months.

"Let's head home," Rafael asked, his voice soft yet filled with unspoken promise.

"Absolutely," Cullum replied.

BACK AT CULLUM'S HOME, THE ATMOSPHERE SHIFTED from public scrutiny to private intimacy, and it was electric. Cullum pulled Rafael into a passionate kiss as soon as they made it through the door. It was a kiss that spoke volumes: gratitude, relief, and overwhelming desire.

Their clothes quickly became irrelevant as they rushed toward the bedroom, eager to shed layers and embrace each other's skin. The air around them crackled with excitement as they fell onto the bed —a tangle of limbs and heated breaths.

Cullum's hands roamed over Rafael's body with awe and desire, tracing every muscle and curve as if committing them to memory. The feel of Rafael's smooth skin under his fingertips sent shivers of delight down his spine.

Rafael responded in kind, his touch both gentle and demanding as he explored every inch of Cullum's rugged form with unabashed enthusiasm. The intensity of their connection was almost tangible—each kiss deepening their bond further, making it stronger and more passionate with every touch.

"Cullum," Rafael whispered, his voice thick with emotion, against his lips. "I love you."

The words hung between them like a sacred vow, affirming everything they had fought for together.

"I love you too," Cullum replied, his voice full of emotion as he pressed another passionate kiss to Rafael's mouth.

———

THEIR LOVEMAKING SESSION WAS AN INCREDIBLE, passionate, and tender celebration of their journey toward self-acceptance and love. Cullum expertly guided his rigid cock into Rafael's eager, gaping hole as the two men pounded away, lost in the pleasure of it all. Every touch was filled with meaning, and every movement echoed the depth of their connection.

As they moved together, their bodies slick with sweat and desire, their world narrowed down to just this moment they were sharing. The rhythm they found was incredible. It was natural, instinctive, and a perfect sync of their bodies' unspoken language. Cullum's thrusts were firm yet gentle, a perfect balance that conveyed both his need and his reverence for Rafael.

Rafael's hands clasped Cullum's shoulders, his fingers digging into the flesh as he arched his back, meeting each thrust with equal fervor. His breath came in ragged gasps, each exhale punctuated by moans that only spurred Cullum on further, driving him wild with desire.

"You feel incredible," Cullum exclaimed, his voice thick with desire as he pressed his lips against Rafael's ear. "Every part of you is incredible."

Rafael responded with a heartfelt chuckle, his eyes twinkling with delight. "I could say the same about you," he whispered, pulling Cullum closer until their chests were pressed together, hearts pounding in unison.

—

THE ROOM AROUND THEM MELTED AWAY, REPLACED BY the incredible sensation of their intense connection. With each stroke, they drew ever closer to the edge, their movements growing more urgent as they chased the crescendo of pleasure.

Cullum shifted slightly, angling his hips to hit that perfect spot inside Rafael, eliciting a cry of pure ecstasy from him. The sound was music to Cullum's ears—a symphony of raw emotion and physical bliss that echoed through the room, making it impossible to contain their excitement.

Their pace quickened, driven by an unrelenting need to reach that pinnacle together—and they did. The air was thick with the heady, intoxicating scent of sex and sweat, mingling with the shared desire between them.

Rafael's legs wrapped around Cullum's waist, pulling him closer and urging him on as they teetered on the brink of the most incredible sensation yet. "Cullum," he gasped, his voice filled with eager anticipation. "I'm close. Let's go for it."

"Me too," Cullum replied, his voice full of excitement. "Let's finish this together."

With one final, powerful thrust, they both exploded in a blaze of ecstasy, cries of release mingling in the heated air as they rode out the waves of their climactic finale. The intensity of their shared orgasm left them breathless and trembling, their bodies still intertwined as they came down from the high in a haze of bliss.

⊂⊃

FOR A MOMENT, THERE WAS ONLY THE SOUND OF THEIR breathing—the rise and fall of their chests as they clung to each other, savoring the incredible afterglow of their union.

www.ingramcontent.com/pod-product-compliance
Ingram Content Group UK Ltd.
Pitfield, Milton Keynes, MK11 3LW, UK
UKHW021523100325

4925UKWH00046B/1111